SAVAGE IN THE TOUCH

SAVAGE HORDE MATES, BOOK 1

MILANA JACKS

ONE

ANDY

S even houses hardly even counts as a village, but since our tavern, which also serves as a bed-and-breakfast, is the last stop before the mountain that travelers must scale on their journey to the capital city, Lyan, we get busy.

The inn is strategically located right at the exit to the valley, and we made sure we put up a sign that says: *No fluffy bed or pillows for another two moons.* Sixty spans is a long time to spend in the forested mountain living in tents. Not to mention, one never knows what kind of criminals lurk in the bushes and what kind of trouble awaits in the mountains.

The road to Lyan is paved with dangers.

Yet that doesn't stop the refugees passing through our little village. They escaped the horde that's been plowing through the south of the kingdom. They say the horde devours everything in its path. They say its hunger can't be tamed.

They say it's coming.

It's all a myth. The "horde" is nothing more than a gang of rebels, or at most our southern fae neighbors looking for trouble. And trouble they shall find, since half a moon ago, the king's army passed through the village on their way south. This means they must already have reached and defeated the horde and are on their way back now.

"Hey, Mag." I greet my sister as I tap my fingernails on the bar, reminding the drunk in front of me to pay up and call it a night. At thirty-seven, I've spent two decades behind this very bar, and I know when the next pint of ale will topple a man. The man isn't chatty, and the ominous threadbare black cloak he wears obscures most of his face, which gives me an impression he came in to drown his sorrows undisturbed. Here's to hoping I won't have to carry his ass up the stairs to the third floor.

Although, if I have to, I will. Third-floor room and board runs at eleven silvers, so a little extra legwork for the guy is included in the price.

"Hey," my sister says and dumps a large bag of potatoes at my feet. "Here you go." She wipes her hands on a dirty white apron fastened to our father's old belt around her waist. Her brown pants will need a wash, as will her white shirt.

I wet a bar towel and wipe dirt from her rosy cheek and neck. "Don't tell me Mike called in again."

"It's past twilight, and I haven't seen him, so..." She shrugs. "Guess he's not coming."

I tuck her golden hair behind her ear and wipe away the dirt over her earlobe. Mag takes after her mother, who might've been a fairy because no other creature in all the lands could be this beautiful, with a pixie nose, smooth skin, perfect round eyes with long eyelashes, and shiny hair that never seems to get damaged or dry, not even in the winter winds.

"Rock, paper, scissors?" I ask. I hate peeling potatoes.

"Sure," Mag says, and we play.

I lose and will have to peel the potatoes early tomorrow.

She winks one pretty green eye. "How did we do for the night?" Mag opens the drawer that holds our coins. A few silvers slide over the wood. Not as many as we need to keep the lights on since the southern rebel problem has cut into our business. Most travelers aren't on their way to Lyan for vacation or business. Instead, they're seeking refuge there, and since most of the south is plagued by the same rebellion that's been going on for over a turn now, the king increased the taxes for the rest of us midlanders and northerners. The tavern and the few rooms we offer upstairs that make up our inn aren't covering the extra cost.

I rub her shoulder. "The soldiers will return."

The drunk lifts his head, showing chapped lips in the shadow of his cloak. He snorts. "They did return."

I frown. "What do you mean?"

"I'm it."

Giggling nervously, I hold out my hand. "Pay up and go rest. Breakfast is served early."

He snorts again. "You and I will be breakfast, and the horde serves itself after dusk."

Mag rounds the bar and sits next to the man. She yanks back the hood of his cloak, and it falls open to reveal the tattered red uniform of a soldier. A lieutenant, judging by the stars on his pocket.

"What happened?" I ask, a tingle of fear making my heart beat faster.

The soldier downs the pale ale and wipes his mouth with a sleeve, rests one foot on the floor, and wobbles as he stands. "The question is what *will* happen."

"What will happen?" I lean over the bar, and my sister leans in too, practically touching him.

He kisses her forehead. "The horde will come. They will consume. They will leave."

I lean back. "What do you mean, consume?"

"They're predators."

My sister and I laugh. We've heard the myth a million times, but our father, the king's historian, has been searching for these creatures for over ten turns, well before anyone ever mentioned them. He kept returning empty-handed, and as punishment, a few turns back, the king chopped off his head.

Now, whenever anyone talks about devastated villages, devoured corpses, and ravenous creatures, they say it's the horde. But if our father found nothing, despite the threat to his life, they don't exist.

"There's no such thing as the horde or predators," I say.

"I saw them." He points to his bloodshot blue eye, and I note the crusted blood under his fingernails. "A creature with teeth the size of my fingers, claws, fur, bright red eyes, ripping through my buddy's guts...and eating."

"Gross," Mag says.

The soldier stumbles toward the stairs. "The horde is coming."

"If they're coming, why are you still here?" I ask. He's full of shit.

"Nowhere to run. The king will kill me anyway. I'd rather my family think I died in battle than have them watch my beheading in the square."

The soldier's footsteps echo in the now-silent bar. The last patrons, a family with a small boy, throw silvers on the table and rush out the double doors.

"Hey," Mag shouts as she runs after them. "Hey, come back! He's crazy. Don't listen to him."

"The horde is coming!" the boy yells, and with that, the refugees passing on the road before the inn scramble. Screaming and yelling ensues as people start trampling one another, surging toward the road that leads to the bridge.

Mag waves her arms. "Stop, stop! There is no horde. It's just people like us playing dress-up."

Grabbing the tray, I start clearing the table, knowing Mag can't stop the madness. The word "horde" throws people into a frenzy. That's because they don't know the king like we do. Our father told us of the king's ruthlessness and that the king would protect his land, if not his people. He wouldn't allow the horde to pillage and seize his land, not after he conquered it with blood and magic.

Besides, the king commands medeisars, creatures of magic nobody can defeat. The predatory horde, even if they weren't a myth (and they are) are no match for those creatures or for the king, who is said to be able to kill thousands with a single sweep of his hand. Father has seen it, and so I believe it.

Despite the danger to his life, my father couldn't find the horde.

They don't exist.

"They're a myth," I say out loud into an empty tavern.

Mag returns, grabs a bottle of our cheapest whiskey, and sits at the bar. She pours a pair of shooters.

We down them, then slam the glasses on the bar top. Whiskey burns down my throat, and I chase it with water.

"Let's clean up," Mag says and starts unraveling her messy braid. "You wake up early and peel the potatoes, and I'll cook breakfast."

"For our one guest?"

She smiles. "And us."

I smile back. "And us."

She presses a warm callused palm over my cheek and pecks my nose. "Me and you, sister," she says. "We keep going no matter what. Right?"

"Right."

"The horde is a myth," she says.

"The horde is a myth. The monsters are a myth," I repeat. No, really, they are.

... UNTIL THEY'RE NOT.

CHAPTER
TWO
ANDY

S creams jolt me out of bed. Mag is already up and running to the window. She parts the curtain, peers out into a moonlit street, and sees something that makes her turn around with eyes wide and terrified.

At the foot of my bed, I freeze. "What is it?"

Mag runs past me and swings open the door, where the soldier stands, holding a blade to his throat.

"I told you so," he says, and slices across his own throat.

Blood gushes down his shirt, staining his uniform pants as he falls to his knees, almost toppling us over.

"Come on," my sister says, tugging at me. I trip over the man as I pass him, and we rush down the stairs faster than when we were little girls and Father would come home from a trip.

At the front door, I jerk against my sister's grip. It's the middle of the night, and I'm scared. "What's out there?"

"Something terrible. Don't look. We'll run for the forest and Blains Peak, to that cave we used to hide in when we were kids. You remember?"

"Yeah." The moon shining through the curtained

window illuminates the side of her face but not much else in the inn.

"We stick together."

"Yeah, you and me, sister. We keep moving."

"That's right." She nods. There's a quiet moment, right before my sister opens the door, when our eyes meet. Hers are filled with determination. Mine are tearing up.

"Wait," I say. "What if we don't open the door?"

"We have to get out of the village."

"What if it's too late?"

"We have to try anyway."

"Just..." I put my palm up while people outside shriek bloody murder. "Don't open the door."

Mag moves her fingers away from the handle and stands next to me. "Okay, Andy, I won't."

We stand in the bed-and-breakfast, staring at the old door that could use a fresh coat of paint, listening to the people's terror. Noises I've never heard before, those of snarling animals gnawing on flesh, reach my ears, and I slap my hands over them.

Mag peeks through the peephole.

Something heavy thuds against the door, and she cries out, then covers her mouth.

We know the moment the monsters hear us, because several of them mimic her terrified scream. Mag and I run across the tavern, behind the bar, and cut a corner to get through the hallway that leads to the back door of the house. We burst through the back door, heading for the bridge that crosses the river, but almost run into a horse near our hitching post. He snorts and shies sideways, then swings his massive head around.

His eyes are red, his teeth sharp and pointy, and blood drips from his muzzle. Taller and broader than our biggest draft horse, he wears no bridle but a spiked breastplate with a circular pendant on it. Other horses from hell like him gallop toward us, all with bloody muzzles and lifted lips so we can see their sharp teeth.

Mag takes a few steps back, and we return into the inn, then close and lock the back door behind us. Heavy footsteps thud across the wood planks inside the tavern, glasses click, and I think I hear someone pouring ale. Mag puts a finger over her lips. I nod. Yeah, I won't make a sound.

We stay and listen. A chair scrapes the floor, and then a glass hits the table. Someone is sitting down and having a drink. I glance at Mag, and her frown reflects my thoughts. What the fuck? But we don't investigate. Maybe the rebels are done raiding and now one of them is having a drink and he'll leave soon, taking all his buddies with him far, far away from here.

Or not, because loud footsteps indicate other men entering, and soon Mag and I have a tavern full of loud men, and probably their animals too, because there's snarling, growling, and a difficult-to-place language that's more like barking than anything else. Mag and I installed a plank wall behind the bar to cut off the hallway view so patrons can't see in the back and also to give the bar more shelf space. The wall blocks their view, or else they'd see us standing here, unmoving.

After a while, when we realize these men must intend to drink all our ale, we sit, our backs to the door in the dimly lit space illuminated only by a small lantern hanging above the exit. Outside, the horses from hell are snorting and galloping back and forth, so there's no way we're leaving. Out front, the tavern sounds full to bursting. We're trapped, but alive, so that's good. I only wish we'd shrugged on robes or coats over our nightgowns.

"Mag," I whisper so quietly, I barely hear myself. "We can't stay here. They'll find us."

"We know you're there," one of them says from the hallway in broken Stenan.

My blood runs cold, and Mag's eyes widen.

They're not from here or from the Stenan Empire. Are they fae? I doubt it. From what Father told us about the fae, I can't imagine the fae drinking in taverns such as ours. Though I can imagine them slaughtering us.

Mag presses a finger to her lips.

I roll my eyes. "They already know we're here."

"We don't have to remind them," she hisses.

"Mag, we're screwed."

"I'm hoping if we stay quiet and give them whatever space they need, they'll spare us and get on their way."

"Good idea." And in fact, they haven't approached us.

Mag and I spend the better part of the night against the door, listening to the males out front celebrate what I presume was their raid and kill.

"Mag, what if I need to pee?"

"Do you?"

"Not yet."

She stays quiet.

I still think we're screwed, so I carry on. "If I piss on the floor, would you clean it up?" I hate housekeeping. Which is awkward given that I'm a professional housekeeper, but lots of people dislike their jobs and are stuck with them anyway because they put food on the table. If it were up to me, I'd travel the world like my father until I died somewhere when I reached the end of it, if there is such a thing as the end of the world. Much more appealing than scrubbing floors, cleaning up after other people, and peeling potatoes.

Mag purses her lips. "Rock, paper, scissors?"

We play, and I lose again. "What is up with you and winning this span?"

"My lucky span." Mag's smile doesn't reach her eyes, and she swallows.

"Don't worry. We spent hundreds of gold on our plumbing, so I won't go on the floor."

"That's for the guests," she says. "You have to go outside."

We chuckle. It's an inside joke. Even after installing plumbing and several waste rooms, Mag and I still go out back to the old shed to do our business. Old habits die hard.

Suddenly, everything grows silent. You could hear a pin drop in the bar. Have they left and we were too busy yapping to notice?

Mag turns and peeks through the crack in the back door, then shakes her head, telling me the horses are still there, so these men haven't left. I have a bad feeling about this.

"Females." The same voice as before calls to us, his accent, thick and harsh on the ears, making our beautiful language sound as barky as theirs. "We have gold for the rooms."

Mag's eyebrows shoot up.

"And for the ale."

"What the fuck?" I hiss.

"But we're out of ale. Bring more ale in ten... nine...eight..."

Mag's green eyes are so wide, they might pop out of her head, and she's stuck in this frozen state while the man counts.

"Four," he says and pauses to say something in his tongue. Another male voice answers, this one deep and foreboding, as if it's coming from the depths of the well. Or hell.

"Coming!" I shout. I scramble to my feet, and Mag and I start pushing the extra barrel we store out back toward the tavern, our eyes focused in front of us, neither of us knowing what to expect as we round the corner.

Behind the bar, we remain crouched until Mag lights a candle so we can see to connect the barrel to the pipes. We hold hands and then rise to our feet behind the bar.

These men have sat in the dark the entire time, and we can barely see anything.

But we can see enough.

"Holy Ensna," I say, and almost release my bladder.

About a dozen pairs of red eyes glow in the shadowy tavern, and as my sister walks around lighting the lamps, I start seeing these men who are not men at all. Like their horses from hell, the males have large red eyes that lift in the corners, and hands with fingertips that end in red claws made for mauling. They wear leather kilts and pants and belts from which people's fingers, ears, and even a foot hang like pendants. Some males have fastened axes over gold breastplates, and others sport red painted stripes on their faces.

And sigils have been imprinted on their skin.

Mag lights the oil lanterns while I stand behind the bar, glowing red eyes watching me.

We, the king's people, don't carry magic. Men who wield magic are called miners and serve the king, fighting the king's wars under a single sigil called the King's Seal. I've never heard of any other kind of sigil, but I know one when I see one. It's a circular thing like a plate that holds a

SAVAGE IN THE TOUCH

magical inscription inside. The inscription describes the type of magic it can execute.

Most often, the King's Seal is on a metal plate or a piece of jewelry like a ring. Sometimes it's a painting kept indoors either on display or in hiding, depending on who has it and how powerful it is.

These...males have sigils with strange symbols on their skin and wear King's Seals as medallions hanging from their belts. I think the seals must have been taken from the king's males who they've slain on their way here, on their way to wherever else they're going.

I hope they go on their way soon.

THREE

The king's female who runs this tavern in the village we raided stands behind her bar as if the barrier will offer her protection while the blonde lights lanterns. We're creatures of the night, with night vision, whereas the king's people aren't. As the blonde approaches my table, which is tucked nicely in the corner by the door, and sets the lantern above me on fire, I get a better whiff of her. Mmmm, she smells nice.

I grab her hip.

She yelps but stays put, her heart a loud banging in my ears. I lift her small hand and sniff her wrist and I'm opening my mouth so I can lick and taste her when something flies through the air. Nimbly, Kasei catches the object and examines it. It's a potato.

"I saved your life, Alpha," Kasei says, and my horde laughs.

"That's a first," I say.

Releasing the blonde with a tap on her hip, I grab the potato from Kasei and bite into it, but almost choke on the terrible taste. We're carnivores. We prefer freshly hunted raw meat that we eat while the blood is still flowing through the prey's veins. The taste of a vegetable makes me want to puke. I swallow the bite anyway and lick my pointy teeth.

I stand and go around the bar to approach the brunette, who's got a knife in her shaking hand. I catch her wrist and squeeze, gently so I don't break her arm, but firmly too, because I can't die at the hand of a barmaid. I have more glamorous plans for how I'm gonna die, and I can only do that after I defeat her king and retake the city of Lyan, the capital of our land, which they now call the Kingdom of Kilselei.

Kilselei belongs to my people. These people in the village? All descendants of Stenants who migrated here after the king purged the land of my people, the Kilseleians. I don't mind the current Stenants, who kneel before my horde. I only mind those who pick up weapons or run from us. Runners spread news and eventually become soldiers who return to fight my horde. I like to get ahead of my kill.

Since these two ladies spent the better part of the night in the back, I took it as a sign they would serve my horde. After all, everyone else either ran or fought, while the females stayed.

A brave, smart choice.

The knife hits the ground, and the brunette fists her small hand. I sniff her wrist. Her scent strokes my senses like a lover, awakening my dick from hundreds of turns of slumber. I lick her skin from wrist to elbow. She tastes like honey with a tang of fresh-cut orange. I want to eat out this girl.

"Get upstairs," I say in Kilseleian, then release her wrist.

She frowns, not understanding me.

I hate speaking Stenan. It glorifies the king's rule over

my people. Also, my Stenan is rusty and likely very outdated, since the last time I walked these lands was over two centuries ago. Times have changed, and my horde and I are adjusting as we travel and raid.

I point up the stairs. "Upstairs. I want to fuck you."

"We don't understand you," the blonde says, then rushes up to the brunette. They interlace their fingers and hold hands. These two are sisters. My sisters would hold hands too, and the memory of them just makes me want to destroy the king even more.

I glance at Kasei, and he translates what I said.

The brunette barks a *no*, rejecting my kind offer of sex. Naturally, I'm offended she'd reject a ride on my fine cock, and in front of my males, who're snickering at her refusal.

"Take me instead," the blonde says.

Now, I haven't spoken or heard much Stenan in over two centuries, so I double-check with Kasei, and he confirms what the blonde uttered.

"Ask her if she thinks I hadn't already decided which one I'm gonna fuck before I spoke."

Kasei translates, and the blonde grits her teeth. "You are welcome to all the ale we have, all the rooms, and the breakfast. Hell, we'll butcher our last pig for lunch if you want, but you can't have my sister." She swallows. "Please."

"I don't drink while hunting kings. I don't need fancy beds. And I already ate your pig."

My males laugh while Kasei translates.

"Then you'll only get breakfast," the brunette says, her voice a whisper over my dick. It tugs something inside my chest, maybe even in my cold heart, for I have no feelings for the king's people.

I smile my best sexy smile that shows my clean white teeth and hides the sharp edges she fears. "Come upstairs with me. You'll have a grand time. I swear on my ax." I grab her hand and yank her away from her sister, intent on kissing her before I throw her over my shoulder, but she presses her palm against the middle of my chest and pushes.

Magic seizes my body, lifts me off my feet, and throws me across the room. I break the table, hit the wall, and, at the last moment before landing on my ass, plant my feet. Ripping the fur cloak away from my chest, I stare at the mating sigil.

It's burning brighter than the lamps.

It's heating my chest like a fire.

In the mirror, my eyes are golden, not red.

Holy Yerlenia, goddess of love, this Stenan female is my mate.

I have a female to court. To court and to conquer! I smile and say in her tongue, "I'm definitely fucking you now."

CHAPTER
FOUR
ANDY

I f the brute creature from hell wants to have sex with me, he will, and there's nothing I can do about it, but I'll be dammed if I'll go down without a fight. That's what I was thinking when I pushed him away. I didn't expect he'd end up on the other side of the bar.

When I touched him, intent on pushing him away, his weight was featherlight on my palm. I stare at my hand, examine it, turn it back and forth a few times, check the other one.

All the same.

"I'm definitely fucking you now," he said.

This is not my first challenge with a man who wants sex. (Is there a man who doesn't?) Some soldiers, especially after they've had a few drinks, start behaving like assholes, demanding sex when none is offered. "I've dealt with guys like you before, and as you can see, I'm not as helpless as I look." I totally am, and I have no idea if I can repeat the miracle push, but I would do it again. Maybe that sigil at the center of his chest is the chink in his armor. I probably injured it somehow, pressed something the wrong way, and it hurt him. Now that I know, I'll do it again if he tries to force me.

The male growls, "The guys you dealt with, I eat for breakfast." He rubs his belly, and the males laugh.

Holy fuck, the rumors are true. The horde are predators, and they eat other creatures.

"We have valuables," my sister says.

The male chuckles and leans an elbow on the stair rail. "I tell you what," he says to Mag, his accent heavy, his pronunciation harsh. I barely understand him. "You show one of my males your valuables while your sister shows me my room for the night. You offered a room, didn't you?" Clearly used to people obeying his orders, he climbs the steps.

If I follow him upstairs, he'll do whatever he wants with me.

If I stay downstairs, he'll do whatever he wants with me.

Upstairs, at least I won't be shamed in front of his horde, and my sister won't have to watch. Besides, I might be able to do that thing where I push at the lit-up sigil on his chest again, and maybe he'll back off completely.

"We did promise them a room," my sister says.

"We treat them as guests, and as with all guests we dislike, we pray their stay is short."

Mag hugs me. "You scream bloody murder if he tries anything. I'll come and...and..."

I rub her back. "And perform oratory slaughter while beating him with Father's Big Book." We kept Father's library the way he left it, including this one book in a language we couldn't read that we call the Big Book. It's the biggest, heaviest book in all the lands.

Mag retreats behind the bar and lines up a dozen shooters. "You boys scared of rum?"

The one who spoke with us sits at the bar. "Baby, rum gives me more power."

They click their glasses together and down the nasty liquor, and Mag pours more. She'll drink a sailor under the table, and she plans to get these males drunk, then slip them a sleeping herb or two. I'm wishing I'd thought of that as I follow the horde male up the stairs, where I find him crouching over the dead soldier.

"This way." I climb all the way to the third floor and unlock the room, opposite the soldier's.

I swing open the door and stand aside.

The horde male ducks as he enters and stands in front of me. As he looks around, I watch him. His nose is large and straight and flares out slightly as he turns up his head and sniffs like that one lone wolf that stops by the tavern during winter. I just hope this male hasn't come here for food.

"You find the room to your liking, I suppose," I say.

The male grunts and walks to the window, peering through it while at the same time kicking the round barrel bathtub with his foot. "Show me to the water." He exits and heads back downstairs as if he knows where the water is or as if he knows I'll do what he says right away. Likely the latter. I peek out the door and find him tapping his foot at the bottom of the steps. His eyes have turned back to red again. I like them golden. They're less frightening.

"Why are your eyes changing color?" I ask as I pass him on the way down.

"Because they do."

"Oh, that makes sense."

He chuckles as we pass the bar where Mag's horde boys

are all set up with their own bottle of hard liquor. She gives me a quizzical look, and I shrug. "He wants to bathe."

Out back, the row of hell horses are lined up perfectly as if they're awaiting their masters. One of them, the biggest one, of course, approaches the male and rubs his cheek against the male's shoulder. The male strokes the horse's neck and whispers into his ear, and the horse whips his head around and stares at me. Those haunting eyes the same color as the horde male's eyes make me uneasy.

I look away and see that the cart Mag and I put together from planks to help us fetch water is broken. I sigh and grab two buckets. "The river is not too far."

"You will take the horse," he says.

That is not a horse, and there's no way I'm riding it, because it might gallop my ass straight to hell. "Before you destroyed our cart, we used to fetch water on foot, so I'll walk." I carry the buckets toward the river, hearing him juggling his own buckets behind me.

At the river, the strong current gushes water into the buckets, and I'm careful not to slip and plunge in. The current would kill me if I slipped. Once I'm finished filling my two buckets, I stand behind the male as he bends to fetch the water. If I lifted my foot and kicked him in the back, he'd fall, and the current would take him away.

I bend my knee just as he turns and walks up to me with a smirk. Gold flecks dance in his eyes as he says, "Lift that foot again and I'll tie your legs around my neck." He snatches my two water buckets from me and walks back up the hill toward the inn.

"I hope you dislocate both your shoulders," I mumble under my breath.

The male carries the heavy buckets to the inn and up the three floors as if they weigh nothing. He then returns three more times until he's filled his bath with twelve buckets. The others he leaves outside. Why I thought he'd injure himself carrying anything is beyond me. He's two heads taller than me, and his shoulders are wider than the door. In fact, he barely squeezes through it, but he does that with a familiar grace, as if expecting everything he passes to be small and dainty, unfit for him. Or his ego.

In the room, I pass him the towel. "Whenever you're done hording around, Mag and I would like to hire you."

The male laughs, a booming, raspy sound.

"Good night," I say and head out. There's a sigil imprinted on the door, carved into it as if it's always been there. It's not the King's Seal either. I tug the handle, but the door won't open. Spinning around, I fist my hands. "No means no."

"I understand no," he says.

"Good. Why is the door locked, then?"

"Because I will spend some time with you."

"I thought you understood no."

"I do. You will help me bathe. It's no less and no more than you've already done with other guests, isn't that right?"

"Sometimes." But those guests weren't the horde from hell. Or as imposing as this male. Or even this hot. I can say what I will about his attitude and assholery, but the male is ripped, strong, and handsome. The epitome of masculinity and sexual vibrance. It doesn't help that I find his accent hot as all hells. I don't want to see him naked.

"Don't be afraid. My cock doesn't have teeth. Come undress me and see for yourself."

Unladylike, I snort, and walk to him. We stand beside the window, and the moonlight makes it easier for me to see what I'm doing. I yank the leather string holding the fur coat he's wearing. It falls on the floor and reveals the golden sigil underneath, the color dim but still bright in contrast to his tanned skin.

My palm itches, and I feel the need to touch the sigil again. It's a pull, almost like a lure. I trace the marking inside the sigil with my finger. "This is a magical sigil, isn't it?"

When the male doesn't answer, I look up. His eyes are golden, his lips parted, and his head dips as if... He rubs his cheek against mine, the way a lion might greet his cub. He smells like something warm and inviting, like spiced cinnamon burning over sandalwood. He reminds me of winter nights spent under furs in front of a fireplace, and when he speaks into my ear in that language of his I don't understand, it doesn't sound barky anymore. It's an invitation to touch him.

I do. I press my palm against the sigil. This time, it does nothing to move the male. Instead, the male inhales sharply and starts purring from his chest.

I gasp and jerk my hand away, then step back. Wild cats purr like that.

"The sigil doesn't lie," he says.

"Are you spelling me? What did you do to me?"

"I did nothing."

"But you wield magic."

"I do."

"How?"

"Very easily."

"You know what I meant." I tug the buckles of the seven leather belts over his belly and release them. The belts fall, crashing all his weapons onto the floor. I spot a machete and pause.

"You want to bleed me?" he asks.

23

"What? No." Well, maybe.

"Then don't look at my blades with longing in your eyes. That look is reserved for my cock."

Unwilling to indulge in his flirting or whatever he thinks he's doing, I shake my head. "Only the fae are born with magic." *Right?*

"Is that a question?"

"No, I know about magic." I know nothing of the sort.

"I smell lies."

"Seriously?" The kilt hangs so low on his hips that it's showing me his pubic hair. When I don't remove the kilt, the male flicks the side of it with a red claw. The kilt falls like a curtain at the end of a theater play. And there it is, his almighty cock rising to greet me and show off the sigil marking at the huge mushroom top of it. It's identical to the sigil on his chest, except this one isn't gold.

"Are you longing for it yet?" he asks as he brushes past me.

Water splashes as he enters the tub. I stand there, staring at the place he vacated, wishing I hadn't said no in the first place, for I can't remember the last time a man touched me. Life has been busy, and I've spent most days in dirty rags with dirty hair, smelling like booze, potatoes, grease, and pig shit.

I still smell like booze, grease, and pig shit, but this asshole, who'll be out of my hair at dawn, is still flirting with me. And that's even after I threw him into the wall.

"If I want to leave the room, would you unlock it?"

"You don't want to leave. The sigil doesn't lie."

"What's your sigil have to do with me?"

"It's not my sigil."

M y mate's life has been hard. If I couldn't already tell how hard by the three calluses on her right palm or the chapped skin at the tip of her thumbs, then I would have known just by looking at the inn. The old doorjambs barely hold even older doors, and the entire establishment needs at least three coats of paint.

The life she's led until now will serve her well on the road to Lyan and after.

I would have left her with gold coins and a big smile on her face. Thankfully, the goddess of love intervened and saved me from myself. I'll still fuck her hard, but I'll treat her like my queen, which means I can't offer her gold in return even if she's in need of coins. Instead, I will court her and earn the burning in her chest when the mating bond between us links us for life and the sigil returns to its rightful owner. Her.

The king's people don't have magic. If they wield magic, it's unnatural and dark and drives them to madness. But there are mates around this land who our goddess has marked for us to serve and protect. She is mine to serve and protect, and the sigil on my chest proves it. It's this female's mark, the mark that tells me I am her savage beast, the mark that reveals her true feelings and desires to me.

My dick's leaking fluid not only because I need to fuck her, but also because she's aroused by the sight of my body.

I knew she would be. The bath served its purpose. I don't need fancy baths. I could've taken a quick swim in the river.

When the goddess first created us, she made us for her pleasure, therefore everything about us is appealing, pleasant on the eyes. It's the same goddess who made the fae. She just fucked them up because fae males are much uglier than my kind. I'll take the whiskers on my ears any span over the fae's pointy ears.

My mate sits on the bed, her hands folded in front of her as she eyes me warily. "Whose sigil is it?" she asks.

I chuckle. "I'll tell you if you help me bathe."

"You don't need help bathing."

"True, but I could enjoy your touch."

It's her turn to chuckle. "You know, for an asshole, you can be real smooth."

"I would have paid you for sex."

"Oh okay, that's much better. You think I'm a whore."

"Inns with taverns often have whores. It's the point of such places. Is that no longer the case?"

She shakes her head, but stays on the bed, now staring at the wall. "Swear on your magic and goddess and whatever you believe will curse you that you won't hurt my sister or me, and I will wash you more thoroughly than your mother since you were a baby."

Her cheeks color as she says it, and she stares at the wall.

"I swear it."

"Can you vouch for your males as well?"

I lift an eyebrow. "Guess."

"I guess you can."

"Mm-hm." Done chatting, I flick two fingers. "Come, female, touch me."

She stands and grabs the cloth and wets it in the bath. "You didn't let me heat the water."

The fire sigil flashes and heats the water, releasing steam into the air. The heat relaxes my muscles, and I groan, then lean my head back, leaving my neck exposed. I wonder why the fuck I'm leaving my neck exposed for a female I just met, even if she is my mate. I take a few moments to contemplate my position and decide I'll give her a chance at cutting me, if only to test if she would dare.

Something pokes my throat. I think it's my knife. The boot one. It's tiny, but cuts all the same. Licking my lips like I'm gonna lick her pussy, I chuckle.

"If you try anything, I'll bleed you like last turn's pig." She means it too, because the sigil on my chest starts burning. This is not what I had in mind when I dreamed of meeting my mate. I dreamed that one full moon, I would meet my mate somewhere deep in the woods. Instantly, she'd bend forward with her ass up so I could mount her and satisfy our mutual lust for each other. She would then, also instantly, love on me, and I would eject the sigil on my cock while I fucked her. It would brand her womb and solidify our mating bond forever and ever. Glory!

But no.

Apparently, the goddess decided she'd make mating a female hard for me.

Not only is my mate one of the king's people, essentially my enemy, but also unwilling to mate. Does she think I'm ugly?

"Do you think I'm ugly?" I ask. If so, I shall capture a fae fucker and force him to throw some pretty glamour at me until I win my mate. After she's mine, I can get back to being ugly all I like.

"Yes," she says, but her scent gives her away. It's a lie. I lick my lips again because my appetite for my mate's pussy grows with each passing moment she's not actively riding my face. I lift my head as she begins washing my arms first, her left hand still holding the knife at my throat. Her right hand touches my biceps like she's massaging my cock, and I suppress a groan, wondering what it will feel like when she does massage my cock.

Eventually, she will. For now, I'll settle for scraps of her attention. Meh. It pains my ego to have to settle, but settle I will.

Sitting on the edge of my tub, she leans over the bath to wash my other shoulder and practically lands her tits in my face. I move my head forward, my face almost touching the globes.

The tip of the dagger pierces my skin. Blood spills and trails down my throat. Her readiness to kill turns me on something fierce, and I purr loudly and use magic to slightly tilt the floor under her feet. My mate slides, tits landing right in my face.

Before I can blink, she straightens herself back up, a pretty blush coloring her face.

"Did you feel that?" she gasps.

Yes, I felt your tits. "What?"

"An earthquake."

Mmhm.

I nudge the floorboards again, harder this time, making the water splash all over the female and tipping her body right into the bath. Her scream is muffled as she dives head-first inside and comes up, arms flailing. Trying to stand, she slips and lands on her ass in the tub. Across from me, her eyes wide and her hair all wet and over her face, she looks like a confused wet kitten, and I am an evil motherfucker. Surely the goddess will punish me for trickery, yet I care less that she will when I lean in and tuck my mate's hair behind her ears. "Stay. Bathe. It's nice and warm, and nobody will hurt you." I leave the bath and get down on all fours to shake the water off, then stand to grab a clean cloth.

I sniff the three soaps the women offer the guests. All are made of pig fat, but have flower scent variations. "Pick one," I say.

"Lavender."

I lather up the cloth and sit on the edge of her bath, then grab her hand and make her rest it on my thigh. My dick's spurting semen now, her hand right near it. The female's head is turned the other way.

I let her play the shy virgin or whatever the fuck she's playing at. The female is mature, over thirty turns, so I know she's seen a man before, albeit a less forward man with a small dick and no charm, or else she would have married by now. Good for me. I can show her a big dick, if not charm. The sigil tells me she's aroused and wants me, and I'll settle for that. For now.

"What's your name, female?"

"Andy. Andreana."

"Tolei," I introduce myself, trying to think what else I can talk about. I've never had to work hard to fuck and never had to win a mate, so I'm discovering new territories as I go, the same way the horde discovers the rules of a new world as we plow through it. Except, I was born to raid and now to retake what was stolen from my people but I wasn't made for chatting.

Thinking for all of five seconds, I decide that if I wasn't born for chatter, I'll shut the fuck up and wash the female and let her chat if she wants to.

Moments pass in silence, and I am oddly content with washing her hand, neck, and cheeks, because the soaked clothes cover the other parts of her fine body.

Big tits.

Tapered waist.

Large bottom.

That'll feel nice under me some night.

Maybe even tonight, since the female starts unbuttoning her white shirt. As if I don't notice what's happing in the tub, I let go of her palm and start unbraiding her long brown hair. The moment I release it from the braid, I run my claws through it from the scalp all the way to the floor.

Andy makes a noise that sounds like a baby wolf growl. Not knowing how to interpret this noise, I continue combing her hair with my claws. The female throws her shirt on the floor, followed by her pants. *Shut the fuck up and claw at her hair, Tolei.*

Her hair is fine, soft, and smells of lavender soap. I bring it to my nose and inhale. Mmhm.

She makes the growling noise again. I still have no idea what it means, but don't dare ask for fear it'll break the spell. Not the magical one. No, this spell is between two mates whose paths finally crossed. I enjoy her quiet naked company and the hitch in her breath as I touch her neck, trailing my claw down her breast, circling the areola, flicking the hard nub that's begging to be sucked. Not by me, but by the baby I'm gonna put inside her.

I squeeze my balls. Hard, so the pain stops me from

doing what I really wanna do: bend her over and fuck her. The urge to mate is strong, and I'm a beast, prone to acting on instincts, not on reason or to comply with female sensitivities.

When I get to her belly, she grabs my wrist and looks up, her brown eyes sparkling with gold flecks, telling me without words that she feels the magic of her sigil.

"Lean into the magic," I say, my voice rough, my speech barely sounding like a man's.

She looks away and pushes my hand between her legs.

I want to flip a cartwheel like a circus monkey, but settle for a mental victory dance. The lack of hair on her mound shocks me, but as soon as I touch my mate's pussy, I care about nothing else besides how I'll make her come. Saliva coats my mouth, and I swallow, then close my eyes and purr as I stroke her moist entrance.

The more I stroke, the more liquid it makes so I stroke her faster, making sure I keep my claws away from her skin. Retracting my claws completely, I dip my middle finger inside and growl when she moans, her head thrown back, eyes closed. It's the perfect opportunity for me to kiss her. I bend, my finger working her pussy, when something slimy brushes against my senses.

I freeze, finger in her pussy, my ears elongating, thin whiskers moving toward the sound like antlers.

Andy clears her throat...and the spell breaks. She moves my hand away from her and jumps out of the tub while I walk to the window, focused on hearing and sensing. Dark magic feels like slime gliding over the wards I erected around the house before the horde decided we'd stay the night.

"Say something," she prompts.

I tap my ear. "I'm listening."

Andy steps between me and the window. "Is there something outside?" She parts the curtains.

"You're blocking my view, so I can't see."

She sidesteps to the left. "Oh, sorry."

I peek through the opened curtains, her face inches from mine. I want to bite her and kiss her and fuck her. "We shall continue with pussy petting some other time." And whoever made me stop will suffer for spans until I tire of torturing them, but I don't say that lest she think me savage. I'm merely annoyed that someone interrupted me.

Andy opens the window and shouts, "Who's out there?"

In utter disbelief, I blink.

She turns to me. "It's just deer or something small."

"How do you know?"

She shrugs. "The horde is in my house. Nobody is coming for logging, that's for sure."

"Maybe if you shout louder so the Zaragans across the seas can hear you, they'll show themselves."

"Well, it was worth trying. You're standing here looking like a statue."

"It is called stealth."

"Oh, I see. Nah, I got none of that."

"Andy," a male hisses from the woods.

She doesn't turn or respond, but I heard him, and I'm gonna kill him. The only way he will survive is if they're of the same blood. I hear the male's boots crunch the leaves, his coat brushing against the bushes. Our horses hear him too, their ears twitching. Mine gets up first, neighs alerting me to an intruder that's approaching my wards.

The male comes from the direction of the river and steps out from under the cover of the trees and into the open yard behind the inn. I wrap my magic around the light in the room and pull it over me like a cloak, so when the male looks up, searching the windows for my mate, he won't see me. I just need to get a good view of his face before I use the edge of my blade to write love letters to my mate all over his cheeks.

Andy leans out the window. "The horde is here! They're here!"

I expect him to spin on his heel and take off, but he says, "I'm not leaving without you. Come on, the soldiers are on their way."

Andy glances at me, looking for something, maybe a signal, and I am truly a statue now because I cannot believe my eyes and ears. These two are conversing about my horde even though she just told him the horde is here. If for no other reason, I'll kill him for his stupidity.

"They're holding us captive," Andy continues, eyes on me.

I motion with my hand. "Please, do go on." I lean my shoulder on the wall by the window, and Andy narrows her eyes. "You can't expect me not to warn my people."

I am her fucking people. "If you show me the same loyalty you've showed that man, I would be honored. The man, however, is wrapped in dark magic, and those soldiers he's talking about are miners who are using him. They're seeing through his eyes, and once they're done with him, he'll be an empty shell, *a messenger*." He reeks of the king's slimy magic. I can feel it all the way up here.

"It's just Mike," she says.

"Is he your brother?" I ask, even though I know the answer.

Andy hesitates, but lies. "Yes, my brother."

In the horde, females protect two things with their lives, their young and their mates, so he must be the mate, because he can't be her young.

I hurl my body through the window and land on my feet before the man. Andy's sigil magic pulses before I have a chance to grab his throat. It compresses my chest, and the pain feels like someone's squeezing my heart. I stagger back when I hear her running down the steps.

Andy's sigil burns my chest, and I want to claw at my skin. She rushes up to me, and the man grabs her hand, extending that slimy magic onto my clean, pure mate. He runs, dragging her away with him, dark magic whispering into her ear that she ought to leave me, the creature of night, the king's magic's mortal enemy.

I run after them, toward the river. She's telling him to stop. She says she can't leave her sister, but he can't stop now. He's already insane, and because he's already insane, he jumps into the river, with my mate in tow.

The strong current sweeps them under.

CHAPTER
SIX

Mike and I sink and tumble at the same time, our hands separating. When I emerge, I swim, but the current carries me anywhere it pleases. Snapping my head back, I double-check to see if my sister may be out of the inn. She is.

Mag is running along the river and screaming my name.

The ripping current takes me under and forces its way into my mouth. I swallow some of it as I claw my way back up. The moment I break the surface and gasp in a breath, the current rocks my body, jerking me left and right.

Alongside me, a male runs down the riverbank, his knees bent backward. Okay, so he's fast, and I'm crazy. Nobody's legs bend that way.

At full speed, I'm approaching the bridge. Gasping when I realize I'll slam right into the pillar of the bridge, I try swimming to the right, but because my mouth is open, water gets in again, and I start choking, panicking because the current is too strong and it's gonna sink me.

Fingers wrap around my biceps, and someone yanks my

body out of the river. Tolei throws me over his shoulder, and I puke water all over his naked ass and a firm thigh that extends into a leg that's definitely bent backward at the knee. He has paws. Paws! But I'm too tired to care or freak out about it. I continue hanging from his shoulder, catching my breath, my cheek resting on his warm back.

The current carries Mike's boot away. I recognize it because it's green with red laces, and because my father gave him the boots many turns ago when Mike's parents left him behind in pursuit of riches in the fae lands. Poor Mike. My eyes brim with tears, though I still hold out hope he'll wash up alive somewhere and start a better life.

Tolei bends his backward knee and leaps from the bridge's pillar all the way to the shore. I lift my head to check out the distance and know for a fact then that horde are predators, and my shame over what happened in the tub, how I let him touch me, warms my face like the summer sun.

As I'm watching his strange leg as he marches back toward my inn, the knee straightens at the same time as the paw becomes a foot. His body is a man's now, and it's as if I imagined the paw and fur.

Male voices drift toward us, and my sister shouts, "Andy! Andy!"

I lift my head. "I'm okay."

"Are you sure?"

"Yeah." I cough. "Fine, really."

At the inn's door, the savage horde predator, a creature of myth and legend, finally puts me down and steadies me by holding my shoulders. His eyes blaze red, and his face is...different, with sharper edges to the bone, and I swear his teeth are larger (if that's even possible) when he shows me them. "I will bend you over my knee."

"That's a really strange thing to say right now."

"It's perfectly sane!" he shouts.

Someone throws pants with a belt loaded with weapons at him, and Tolei snarls, then pulls back his arm and throws his ax. It flies from the back door all the way down the hallway and ends up lodged in the wall partition before the kitchen.

The horde grows silent. Tolei's anger makes everyone look anywhere besides him.

"Nice throw," I whisper, hoping that'll defuse some of his anger.

He points a clawed finger at me, opens his mouth, then closes it, apparently deciding he'll put his pants on first. One leg goes in smoothly, but because Tolei is clearly in a foul mood, he jams the second leg into the pants and tears the stitches right out. He picks up the pants and shreds them into pieces, talking, to himself, likely, in his barky language. Then he walks inside, grabs the whiskey bottle, and starts chugging.

There's something to be said about a naked male with an erect cock standing behind the bar chugging whiskey. Mainly, this guy needs a room.

"Good idea," my sister says and joins him behind the bar. She grabs a shooter and extends her arm. Tolei pours her a drink. Bottle finished, he drops it into the bin and disappears from view. He returns with a towel and wraps it around my body in a tubelike fashion, catching my arms in the process. I can't move, but I dare not tell him that's not how people wrap towels around their bodies. Tolei is having some sort of moment, and I don't pretend to understand this level of aggression or anger or the animalistic behavior he's exhibiting. The grunting, snarling, and heavy breathing that sounds more like growling than anything else tells everyone to shut up or die.

The male who spoke the most enters the tavern and nods at Tolei. They exchange barks, and the voices escalate. My sister and I edge toward the stairs as the other horde members start filling up the space. The two males, Tolei and the other one, are standing chest to chest, and the growling is growing louder and louder. The other male's leg starts changing its shape. First the paw forms, then the knee simply pops out of the socket and bends backward.

Tolei grips the male's throat, and this time, I see his face change. The jaw extends outward, and the teeth grow along with the nose, but his eyes shrink. A third male, a young one, slaps a hand over Tolei's biceps and speaks with him, the male's voice adjusting and sounding calm and reasonable. He must've said something sane, because the legs of the male Tolei's holding by the throat straighten. Tolei still holds him, though.

"Did you see his legs?" Mag whispers.

I nod.

"They're some sort of magical creatures, Andy."

"Predators, Mag."

"Almost drank me under the table."

"That's a really important detail right now, Mag."

"It is."

"How?"

"Metabolism. They have faster metabolisms. Need a lot to get drunk."

"And what do we do with that information?"

"File it for when we need it."

"We're not gonna need it." I speak louder now for everyone to hear. "Because they're all leaving now."

Tolei releases the male's throat and barks at him. The

horde files out of the tavern in record time. Outside, the hell horses neigh as if the horde's mounting them. Oh, thank the goddess and the Lord King. They're leaving.

"*We* are leaving," Tolei announces.

The way he said *we* sounded significantly different from the *we* I'd think he'd use. Surely he doesn't mean him and me. "Safe travels," I tell him. "It was a pleasure to meet you, and thank you for saving my life." *Good fucking bye, savage predator male with a fine big cock.* I wave.

Tolei shows me his teeth. "You are part of the horde."

"Huh?"

"Pack some shit and throw it over my horse, baby."

"I'm not taking my shit or going anywhere with you."

Tolei snorts. "You don't have to pack, but you'll regret not packing later. And you can walk on out of here, or I can carry you."

I start up the stairs, but the large towel is wrapped so tightly around my arms that I almost trip and fall flat on my face. Tolei straightens me, and I want to bite his hand off as he pats my head.

"I will take care of you," he says. "Hurry along. I can no longer afford the rest."

"Why not?" Mag asks.

"Because your soldiers are hunting us."

I smile. "Good."

Tolei snarls. "We're leaving. Pack."

"No," I yell back. "I'm staying where I am. In my home. You have no right to tell me I'm leaving."

"I have every right," he shouts back.

"Oh, you think stroking my pussy gives you special rights? It's not a marriage declaration, you know."

Mag gasps.

"Shit," I say.

Tolei smirks. "It's not a marriage. Marriages can be broken. What you and I have is a mating bond, impossible to break unless one of us is dead. I don't plan on dying or letting you die, even if you plan on jumping into every river we pass on the way to Lyan. I am your savage, and you are my mate. That out there is our horde." He bends slightly so we're at the same eye level, as if he's speaking to a child. "Pack. Your. Shit."

"I can't."

"You can and you will." The savage grabs Mag and starts dragging her outside.

"What are you doing with her? No, don't touch her!" I struggle with the stupid towel and can't rip it off me. It's impeding my movements, so I hop after him, wanting to grab Mag, try to pry my sister out of his clutches.

The male who spoke the most is waiting outside, and Tolei hauls my sister up onto the male's horse, then returns into the inn. He takes the stairs leading up to the rooms. Mag struggles, but the horde savage holds her, gags her, then ties her with rope.

Oh my king, what is happening? Tolei has wrapped the towel so tightly around me already, knowing I'd object to leaving. I can't run, and neither can Mag. All along, he knew he'd be taking me with him. I'm the idiot who thought they'd stay the night and move on.

A horde male gallops by, whistling in a way that makes me think it's a sign or a code of some sort. I turn to see Tolei jump out of his room's window, dressed and ready with all his weapons, and holding one of my father's sacks.

"You can't take the sack," I say.

"I'm not taking it. You are." A click of a tongue, and his horse arrives and stops before Tolei, who scoops me up and turns me over the horse's withers. He straddles his stallion from hell, and the animal rises onto its hind legs. I kick and scream, cry and curse him until my voice is hoarse and the fight leaves my body.

They came. They ravaged. And they captured me. My life is over.

CHAPTER
SEVEN
ANDY

I awaken lying on the cold, hard ground and immediately jolt into a sitting position. Judging by the few sunrays peeking from between the dense trees and the chill in the air, it's early in the morning. My butt freezing, I pat near me in search of a blanket and find rope tied around my ankle. I follow it to the other end of the rope. Tolei has tied the rope to the pommel of his saddle on his hell horse and left me by a tree while the horse grazes the grass around me.

"Andy, you up?" Mag calls from behind me.

I crawl around the tree, tugging the animal along with me.

On the other side, my sister stands, alive and breathing. Scrambling up, I throw my arms around her and hug her so tightly, I think I might squeeze her to death. I bury my nose in her hair and inhale. It's stinky from whatever she's been through, but it's her stink, and nothing belonging to Mag bothers me. "You're fine. We're fine."

"Surprise, surprise." Mag tucks my hair behind my ears.

Something's not right there. I hand comb my hair and find it's short. "Mag?"

"I know," she says.

"What happened to my hair?" I run my fingers through what's left of my hair again. "I didn't cut it." I love my long hair. What happened to it? It's shoulder length now, like it was when I cut it after we got news of father's beheading ceremony. Back then, I threw my hair into the firepit, hoping Nimsina, the spirit that sails the dead into the afterworld, would accept it as payment for a favor from the undertaker, who would then grow a head for my dad when he entered his domain after the public beheading.

Mag flattens her lips. "He cut it."

I lean in. "Tolei?"

She narrows her eyes. "You're on a first-name basis, I see."

Heat crawls up my cheeks, and I'm sure I'm blushing profusely. "Is he around?"

She jerks her head for me to follow her around the huge tree. Chains jingle, and I look down to see that my sister is shackled to a thick tree branch instead of to an animal. Tolei's horse moves with me, giving me the stink eye, which I'm thinking is his permanent look.

The horde males huddle around a firepit. Massive males, their muscular backs the breadth of two of mine, their necks as large as my thighs. Decorated with fine gemstones, leathers, and beads, their long braids hang down their spines.

Tolei's walking around them, two glowing sigils, one red and one yellow, spinning above his palms. Leaves lift off the ground, and the warm wind that blows my way makes me uneasy.

"What's he doing?" Mag asks.

"How would I know?"

Mag snickers. "Don't deny you and the savage got it on."

"I claim a lapse in judgment." And big-cock lust and also magical spells.

Tolei stops, and the sigils return to their position as imprints on his forearms, losing their color completely. He looks my way.

I tug a lock of my hair. "You're gonna pay for cutting my hair. I'll shave you bald while you sleep."

"But you will sleep with me."

"Fuck you, Tolei."

"Can't now, baby. I'm busy, but I'll return soon."

I flip him the bird.

He flips me two and walks backward, then turns around, pulls his pants down, and shows me his bare ass. The horde laughs while I sit by the tree with my knees pulled up to my chest, seething.

Mag plops next to me with a sigh. "He says he's yours."

"He's not mine."

"You know what I mean."

"Nah, sister, I don't know."

"He saved you from drowning."

"He did not," I hiss. "I almost drowned because of him."

Mag shakes her head. "Let's talk about him and them later. They can hear everything we're saying."

"No way, I can barely hear myself."

"They're predators." Her eyes plead for me to shut up, and so I zip it and stare, trying to silently communicate with her like we used to when we were little girls and Father would make us stand out back in the dead of the night when soldiers would visit and he bartered the king's secrets with them.

The reality of liking the touch of a male predator, crashes into me and makes my stomach queasy. Gulping, I slump against the tree.

Mag takes my hand in hers. "They spared us, Andy. They ransacked the village, but spared our lives. Whatever happens, we're alive right now, and that means..." She pauses, and I wait for her to tell me what it means.

When Mag says nothing, I ask, "What's it mean?"

"Think about it."

"We can escape," I say firmly, because that's the only thing I want to do.

"Shhhh." She presses a finger over her lips. "They can hear us."

"You're paranoid. They can't hear this far out."

"Remember Brolio?" She lifts an eyebrow.

"The dog that one soldier left behind?" And we fostered until we found him a good home.

"Yeah, that one. He was thirteen years old, half-deaf, and yet he could hear you coming from the stable from his corner under the bar."

I nod. "True. He could smell carved ham too. He'd run down the stairs like his tail was on fire when he smelled ham."

Mag chuckles, and we fall quiet for a while, each one in our own head.

I sniff. "What's that smell? Oh, ewww." I plug my nose and then my mouth as my belly rises.

Mag slaps a hand over her mouth and nose just as the hell horse walks up, poop landing in great big dumps all over the green grass. The poop is yellow with red streaks, and I gag and gag, then slump over on the grass. Mag lies with me, and we turn on our sides. She takes my hand and turns up my palm and starts finger writing on it.

I make out a few letters, but can't put them together to make words. "What?" I whisper.

Mag rolls her eyes. "Whispering won't help. They'll hear us."

"I can't make out your sign language."

"Oh my lord, Andy, why are you giving away the way we can communicate without talking? These are signs. I'm showing you our secret signs."

"We have secret signs?"

"We do now." She finger draws on my palm again. I stare at my palm and shake my head.

That gets me another eye roll. Mag stabs my palm with her finger, jabbing the signs now. I wince, but pay more attention this time.

I take her palm and write the same thing I think she wrote. *Night.*

She shakes her head and writes again.

I frown.

She repeats the sign on my palm, her nail making dents in my skin.

"Getting all stabby over there, sister," I deadpan.

She sighs and turns onto her back. "Forget it."

"Just tell me what it is," I whisper.

"They. Can. Hear. Us." She lifts her head, and her eyes widen. "Hush. They're coming."

Tolei touches my ankle. I jerk my leg away, forgetting that I'm tied to the hell horse. The horse protests and tugs back, preparing to take off. Oh no!

I sit up and scramble for the rope as the horse starts dragging me away from the meadow. Tolei barks what I am sure is a command and grabs my ankle, this time not letting me jerk it away.

Instinctively, I pull back my other leg and kick him in

the nose. Blood spurts out of it, and Tolei blinks his red eyes, which, like flames, burn in rage. His chest rises and falls, nostrils flaring. He grinds his jaw and swipes a thumb over the blood and then smears his blood on my cheek. He starts chanting something. It freaks me out, and I try batting his hand away when he swipes my cheek again.

When he won't get away from me, I kick out again, but this time, he captures my other ankle too. Both feet in his one hand, he unties me with his spare hand and starts dragging me away. Mag shouts after him, but he shrugs her off when she can't move past her own shackles.

I scrape the ground with my fingers, digging them into dirt, my gaze on my sister, who's screaming herself hoarse begging him to take her instead. He won't take her. He wants me. He's made that clear, and something about this reminder makes me stop fighting.

The moment I stop, he pauses and offers me a hand to help me stand up.

I get up on my own and look around. We're inside the forest and away from the clearing, but not too far. I still see the tree Mag's tied to. "Release my sister, and I'll do whatever you want."

"You'll do whatever I want anyway, and with your sister traveling with you, you'll be happier."

"You think you know me?"

"Not yet, but I'm looking forward to getting to know you."

I snort. "As if I would tell you anything about me."

"What do you know about that man?"

"Which man?"

Tolei's voice is slowly changing, becoming less like language when he speaks, and more like an animal growling or communicating with other animals. "The man

47

you ran off with," he manages to say. Again, the bones of his jaw now appear sharper somehow and his cheeks more lifted.

"Are you a predator?"

"The man!" he shouts.

"Mike!" I shout back. "His name is Mike, and I know a lot about him."

Tolei breathes heavily as if trying to contain himself. "Don't push me, female," he whispers. "I already know his name is Mike. Nothing new there. I need to learn more about him and who he walks with so that I can find him and rip his guts out while I eat his heart."

"He's probably back home celebrating you all left, or he's dead at the bottom of the river. He was coming to work when you galloped into the village and killed everyone."

"Not everyone," he reminds me. He jerks his head to the left. "My home is this way," he says and walks away. When I walk the other way back toward my sister, he appears in front of me, a big wall of muscular man chest.

"I said my home is this way. I expect you to follow me and not walk in the opposite direction."

"My sister is there." I point. Besides, we're in the forest. Who the fuck lives in the middle of the forest? I don't say that, though.

"I know where she is."

"I'm staying with her."

"You will stay with me."

I shake my head, open my mouth to argue, but he throws me over his shoulder.

"Hey, put me down." I kick and hit his back with my fists, almost hurt myself doing that because he's built like a rock.

We enter a tent. When the tent flap falls, I expect Tolei

to lower me back down, but he spanks my bottom, then sits down himself.

I try wrestling away from him, but it's no use. Maneuvering my body over his knee, he takes my wrists and holds them at the small of my back while his other hand reaches under whatever raggedy dress I'm wearing (what am I wearing?) and yanks up the hem. The bottom of the dress falls over my eyes. Bent over, I try blowing at it and shaking it off. I'm wriggling on his lap when Tolei lands a slap on my bottom that makes me scream.

"If soldiers are around," he says, "they will hear you and come."

I scream louder.

"Is that so?"

"It is so," I say.

Tolei spanks me again.

I'm mad he's spanking me, and he's spanking me because I pushed back against his orders. I'm writhing while he wants me to stay put, but if I stay put, he might figure out this turns me on. Tolei lands two more on my already heated ass cheeks, then rubs them gently, sometimes trailing his palm over the back of my legs, with an occasional brush of his thumb between my thighs.

The more he rubs my bottom and massages my thighs, the more aware of him I become. His pants, for example. They're made of suede and stitched with fine linen that invites me to brush my hand over them. Gently, I do just that, hoping he won't notice.

Tolei starts purring. It's barely audible, an oddly soothing sexy sound. The scent I remember from inside the room back at the inn enters my nose. It's pleasant and masculine and conjures up images of dirty, raw fucking. I bet Tolei is a forceful lover, the kind of male who throws a girl around the bedroom or floor or wall like he owns her body. I bet I would like that.

He purrs louder now, his hand moving between my legs. Just when I think he'll rub my pussy again, he picks me up and sets me on my feet. I stare down at him and his golden eyes, his head leaning all the way back to look up at me while his hand trails up my thigh and parts my legs. Grabbing my hip, he pulls me to stand between his legs.

I spread mine and close my eyes when he sneaks a finger inside my pussy.

"Look at me," he barks.

I snap open my eyes.

He smiles. "We'll finish what I started and get you off now. Hang on to my shoulders and ride my finger."

I rest my hands on his shoulders, and my eyelids flutter as he swipes over my clit.

"Look at me."

Okay! Damn. Eyes wide open and locked with his, my body starts moving over his finger.

"That a girl. I will reward you and give you two fingers to fuck. Fuck them."

The second finger stretches me, and I sigh both from pain and pleasure, again my eyelids fluttering, wanting to close and enjoy this fully.

"Keep 'em open, mate. Face your male. Acknowledge you like my touch. Do you want me to lick you?" He rubs me faster, thumbs over my clit while moving two thick fingers inside me.

"Answer me," he barks.

"Yes!"

"Okay, baby, you don't have to get mad at me." He winks and stands abruptly, grabbing my hips. He lifts me above his head and tucks his face between my legs. Bewil-

SAVAGE IN THE TOUCH

dered, I grab his hair and hold on. He's looking up at me while I'm looking down as he opens his mouth and sticks out his black tongue. It's long and ridged.

"Sit on my tongue."

With my knees resting on his shoulders, and his head titled back, I sit on his mouth. I don't dare close my eyes because his are open and watching me, but I want to. I want to so badly because his tongue feels so good as he moves it over my clit at a speed I can barely handle, and his arms tightly gripping my hips move my body back and forth so I'm practically riding his face.

The patch of beard he keeps on his chin provides friction, and soon I find myself rubbing on his chin, his tongue, the entire bottom of his face. My eyes are closed, but I don't care as he gives me pleasure that accumulates inside my lower belly before I release all over his face.

I grit my teeth against screaming and ride my orgasm for all its glory, then peel open my eyelids to see Tolei's eyes are closed.

He snaps them open, but I caught him.

I smile, and he winks at me.

I like this playful side of him that he shows me briefly.

Tolei settles me on my feet, the sigil on his chest blazing gold.

"Tend to my needs." He drops his pants and pulls back his shoulders, then assumes a wide stance, legs shoulder-width apart, cock standing long and proud, the sigil imprinted on the tip taking on a lighter red hue.

"Don't fear my cock. It has no teeth or claws. It's perfectly hard, and you will like it at the back of your throat, in your pussy or ass, wherever I want to stick it." He takes my hand and makes me grip him. I use my other hand too, because he's thick and wide, and as I move my hands over his cock, Tolei watches me. It's unnerving and so inti-mate, too intimate for me, or maybe too forward or forceful for me. I don't know which. I look away.

Tolei purrs, growls, and grunts while I jerk him off, his cock pulsing in my hand. He touches his balls and rubs them while I rub the sigil on his cock's head. Tolei's breathing becomes erratic, and his nostrils flare.

He grips my dress at the collar and rips it. A moment later, seed gushes out, all of it landing on my breasts and belly while Tolei helps me squeeze him and jerk him off until every last drop comes out of him. Soaked in cum, I stand there watching him breathe more heavily than before, wondering *what now?* He swipes two fingers over my breast and picks up his cum. He puts it in his mouth and then kisses me with that mouth full of his cum.

It tastes like everything decadent I can think of. Dirty fucking in particular.

Tolei steps back and puts on his pants. "Don't wash."

"What?" I frown.

"Leave my seed on you."

"It's sticky and gross."

He lifts an eyebrow. "It's my seed that will grow a baby inside you. There's nothing gross about it."

"Um…" I chuckle, a little hysterical sounding. A baby?

"Leave the seed on the skin so my males can smell it. It will save their lives and the lives of many others. Perhaps even your little boyfriend Mike."

"You're jealous."

"I'm maniacally jealous. Keep that in mind, mate. The lives of…the other males in the lands depend on how you handle me and my feelings."

"Your feelings."

"Yes, feelings. I have them. We all do, something your people have forgotten, and mine will soon remind them of."

"What are you talking about?"

Tolei pinches his lips. "Nothing." He bends as if to kiss me, and I even turn up my face, but he brushes his cheek against mine. It's such an animalistic thing to do, but it's also unique and interesting and maybe also endearing.

Wind whooshes past the flap, which we didn't secure, and blows out the small candle illuminating the tent. I can barely make out a seating area made of fur and logs on my left and a curtained room in the back. Made of stitched and braided leather and beads, the curtain gives the tent a... homey feel. If he's a horde male, then they travel and move around, and this is his home.

The chairs and logs and even the rugs are all mismatched, and I conclude those have been looted. Tolei parts the curtain and shows me his bedroom. The bed is made of thick furs and mismatched pillows, and there are weapons hanging above it.

"You will spend the night here," he says, throwing himself onto the furs. Groaning, he leans to the side and reaches for a fluffy red blanket. He shakes it out, smells it, and grunts. "It's good. Blanket?"

"No, thank you."

He groans as he lays his head back down. It makes me think he's tired.

"Are you tired?" I ask.

"I'm never tired."

"Ha! That's what they all say."

Tolei's head whips up, eyes a bright red. "Who are they?"

I sit on the edge of the bed. "I meant the soldiers, warriors, whatever you call yourselves. Men in arms. They

53

come in dead tired, but if I ask about it, they'll deny it. Something they teach in man school."

"I'm not a man, Andy."

I thread my fingers through the soft russet fur under me. I napped on the way here, wherever here is, so I'm not tired. He's nocturnal, and it's daytime, so surely it's past his bedtime. "My sister will need shelter."

"She will have it."

"Promise."

"I do."

"I want to see it for myself."

"You will have to learn to trust me. You will see her later. Blanket?"

I shake my head.

He chuckles. "You'll beg for one later."

Probably. "Never."

Shortly after, I hear soft snoring. No, wait. I listen, stopping my own breathing so I can hear better. In his sleep, he purrs. Slowly, I stand and tiptoe to the exit, then peek through the flap and extend a foot outside.

"Mate, I can hear a mouse digging a burrow on the other side of the meadow."

"Oh, so you do have super hearing."

"Yes."

"Okay, thank you for the confirmation."

"Anytime. Sit back down, or I'll tie you to my horse again."

Well, that would suck. I return to sit by the bed. Soon thereafter, I grab the blanket and snuggle under the furs, hoping he's a male of his word and will provide shelter and protection for my sister.

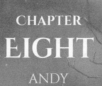

CHAPTER

EIGHT

ANDY

T hree spans later, Mag and I are alive and well, traveling through the thick forest with the horde, my savage keeper sometimes walking beside me, most often walking at the front of the group. The horde hasn't hunted inside the forest for the three nights we've stayed with them, nor have they slept at night.

At first, I was too proud to ride his horse because it's something the savage offered as a courtesy, but now I'm happy he forced me to ride it. I wouldn't have been able to keep up with the horde's long strides or their stamina. For three spans now, they've walked from dusk to dawn, taking one or at most two rests, and most of those rests are for my sister and me when we ask to stop for a bathroom break.

My sister travels with Tolei's second-in-command or whatever the male Tolei spends the most time with is called. I'm unsure if the horde has ranks, and they mostly speak their own language, so I can't understand, although I'm learning some words as the spans roll by. They curse a lot, and so that's what I've learned. I'll throw one or two curse words at Tolei just to make him laugh. Laughter looks good on him.

And there's something about the moon. They keep looking up through the dense trees as they march toward Mount Havensi, the place the moon hides behind. Or at least that's how most children's tales start. *"Once upon a full moon that hides behind Mount Havensi, there lived..."*

Whenever we get a bathroom break, I scout for an escape route. The problem is that not only can they hear everything, but they're alert, intelligent, and fast, with bodies made for endurance running. We wouldn't get two steps out before they noticed.

The horde males don't tire after walking these three spans. On the hell horse, I close my eyes for a moment, and my body sways. I lose balance and feel myself falling, and just barely catch the reins at the last moment so when I hit the ground, I don't break my neck.

Everyone stops. I just lie there, eyelids fluttering closed.

"What are you doing now?" Tolei asks from somewhere above me.

Eyes closed, I answer, "I'm going to sleep."

"We haven't reached the mountain yet."

"Yeah, and?"

"And we have not reached the mountain yet."

"But we've reached a consensus that you like to repeat yourself."

"Actually, I dislike it. It's only with you that I'm having to repeat myself."

"Don't bother. I don't listen well."

Tolei picks me up and throws me over the animal's back as he's done several times before, but this time, he sits on the saddle with me and arranges me on the horse so I'm sitting sideways, my head resting on his hard chest. I'm okay with that because, pressed like this, I hear the low purr that I listen for at night. It's faint in the daytime, but it's there as he breathes. Oddly, it comforts me and makes me feel safe.

And so onward we travel.

CHAPTER
NINE
TOLEI

The most awkward moment of my life happened on the way to the mountain. One moment, I was planning the overthrow of the king's position we're about to hit, and the next, I found myself holding a female against my chest and leading my horde away from the king's position and into a cave at the base of the mountain for rest.

Confused males give me *what the fuck are we doing here?* looks as they settle into the cave, each one as far from the other as possible. The cave's large, so there's plenty of space for all of us to stretch out and, hell, maybe even rest after a cycle of traveling across the land, during which we rested only a few times.

Maybe we're tired. Who knows? Not me. I'm never tired. Mmhm.

As I scout the cave's large interior, I follow my nose, which leads me past the few hot water ponds my males have already claimed and deeper into the cave. Ice drips on the slippery floor, and I watch my step as I carry my mate close to my chest.

I could do this all span long. Having her near the mating

sigil soothes me and should bring her closer to me, the magic that binds us drawing her in, easing her into an acceptance of our bond that I intend to seal during a full moon.

My female's sister follows behind me, her shackles making too much noise. I don't like the shackles, but she's not my female, so I haven't said anything. Until now. Now, the noise grates on my ears as it echoes off the walls.

"Tell Kasei I said to remove your shackles." I push farther into the cave, where I sniff out water and a pleasant smell. Maybe plants that grow in the dark. Hm. I follow my nose left and into a tunnel.

The female's shackles clink louder behind me as she stumbles in the dark. "Do your males always do what you ask?"

"Yes." We arrive where my nose has led me, a space large enough to fit all the horde but that I'll allow to hold only my mate and me. There's a place for my tent, a tiny river under a few rocks on the left that my horse can drink from, and a hot bath. I place my mate on the ground, then turn back to where her sister waits for me at the tunnel.

"Why are you following me?" The female knows I'll be resting with Andy, and their time together, unless they're using the bathroom, is mostly supervised. I don't trust either of them not to run and die in the woods, and they are not ready to accept that they're part of my horde now.

It has been centuries since any horde that has roamed the lands during the king's rule has had females, and I'm pretty excited mine is first. My brother will be jealous, and I'm looking forward to rubbing it in his face. I'm also looking forward to the moment when he realizes mating is a genuine possibility and not a myth for us anymore. That's gonna require a celebration. A mating ceremony, perhaps?

"You're thinking, horde male," Mag says, reminding me she's still here.

"I am anticipating the future, king's female." I walk toward her, intent on returning for my horse, when she steps in my way.

"What do you see?" she asks, her pretty green eyes like those of a fairy staring up at me with determination. She's after something.

"I see the future I want to create," I deadpan.

She rolls her eyes. "My sister," she says, "is pretty. She is a fine mate for a warrior like you."

I raise an eyebrow. "Are you bargaining or selling her to me?" Clearly, my mate hasn't told her sister what mating means. She might have said something had she actually inquired about the mating, but she hasn't. Mostly, she's ignoring our connection, but she will come around, and my cock will help speed up the process.

Mag frowns, obviously not understanding me. I clarify. "Once upon a time, bargaining with a female meant we'd exchange her for goods. Selling her would be...well, selling her for coin."

"Bargaining," the older sister says, "and those days aren't yet behind us, sadly."

"Write up a complaint and send it to your king," I suggest with a wink.

"Fuck you, Tolei."

"I intend to, Mag. Now, let's pretend you are your sister's keeper, which you are not, and we are bargaining. What do you want in exchange for your sister?"

"I want a good life for my sister."

"Deal."

"A happy life, Tolei."

"Yeah, I heard you." I push past her. Her shackles don't follow me, but her voice does.

"A life far away from weapons, raids, battles, or whatever you're planning next."

At the tunnel exit, I survey the males, who are all mostly asleep apart from a pair that keep watch. We don't like setting up wards this close to a king's position that we intend to raid. They don't know we're coming. The one scout they sent, we diverted with a few tricks we learned on the way here. I didn't get to be this old by having a little scout boy find me in the woods. Please. The king's too arrogant for his own good.

I click my tongue, and my horse enters the cave, followed by other animals. Returning to my territory for the night, I pass Mag at the tunnel entrance and wonder how long she'll stay there. At my horse, who's found fresh water, I swipe the sack and go about constructing my home, keenly aware that the sister lingers at the tunnel's entrance.

"I don't need to justify my ways or my horde ways to you or anyone else," I tell her as I set up the tent. "My mate shall decide for herself."

"She wants to return home. Does that mean nothing to you?"

"I take my home with me, so no."

"She is homesick."

"Sick?"

"Sick."

"She's tired from the road, that's all. She will rest and continue."

"You are incredibly difficult to talk to," she says.

"Not at all. I'm the rosiest fucking flower of the bunch of us. You should meet my brother."

"No, thanks."

I smile. "But you will." Somewhere out there, my sigil, which speaks of my family and our roots, has reached my brothers and woken them, released them from their sleep, telling them I have awoken and am traveling with my horde. They know where to go and where to meet me, for if they don't, if we don't have the numbers we need, the king will kill us all.

I head for Lyan based on faith and a little bit of lunacy.

And my mate is coming with me.

"I am a horde male, and Andy is a horde mate. When our bond is complete, she will have endurance and strength far surpassing that which she was born with." She will also be immortal like me. I don't say that, though, for the knowledge of our immortality prompted the king's envy and greed. It turned him into a madman who searched endlessly for ways to channel our magic. It paid off. He is immortal now, at great cost to my people.

It offends me that my mate is one of his people, but I accepted it because she is mine. However, some of my males haven't and have voiced their concern to me in the same way Mag is protesting now. But in the end, our bond is our business, and everyone else can kiss my nice firm ass.

"You may leave us now," I say in a voice very few argue with.

Mag leaves, those loud chains Kasei's insisting on putting on her grinding against my nerves. I hope she remembers to tell him I said to get rid of them so I don't have to do it myself. She is his captive, and I wouldn't want to meddle in a male's claim on a female he caught after the raid. It could get bloody, a fight we should avoid.

CHAPTER
TEN
ANDY

For the first time in several spans, I awake warm and with my nose buried in bedding made of fur. I rub my face in the softness and sniff, trying to tell which animal fur I'm using before my brain catches up and asks why I'm under the furs in the first place.

With that thought, I snap open my eyes and peek through the covers. Tiny lights illuminate an uneven ceiling with icicles formed in high places. The hell horse huffs near me, his warm breath getting lost in the cold air. We rest in a cave.

Tolei lounges inside the steaming pond, his back to me, elbows propped at the edge, his hair blocking the view of his back. Under the covers, I'm fairly certain I'm naked. Double-checking by running my palm over my naked belly, I look for my sack, the only item of mine he's brought with him.

Sitting up, I drag a fur over my breasts. "Is it nighttime?"

Tolei spins, and the sharp turn sweeps his hair to the side, revealing a soft brown braid. Is that my hair? It can't be. Blurry eyed and disoriented, I rub my eyes, then stare at him, waiting for an answer.

Tolei smiles, showing me all his teeth. His red eyes lift and crinkle at the corners. "You're very cute when you wake up. Makes me want to pet you."

"Like a horse."

"My horse doesn't have a pussy I'd want to pet."

I hide my smile by dragging the fur over the bottom half of my face. I don't want to encourage him, though his bluntness entertains me. I also enjoy knowing where I am with him. There's no doubt he wants to fuck me. He's after me with the full force of his being, and his being is pretty forceful and persistent. Coyness seems a foreign concept to him.

"Brokko isn't cute," Tolei continues. "He's a fierce animal, and cuteness would offend him."

The horse huffs, gets up, and walks away. I half expect him to take a shit in protest or confirmation of what Tolei is saying.

"Does he understand us?" It sure seems like it.

Tolei pauses before answering. It's a tiny fraction of hesitation, but it's unusual for him to pause, which makes me think he might lie.

"He senses we're talking about him."

"How?"

Again, Tolei pauses, scrubs his beard, gaze briefly on the ceiling before he points at the sigil near his wrist. He traces the small sigil with one red claw. "We are connected, Brokko and I, as is every horde male with his animal."

"Connected by magic?"

Tolei nods.

"In the same way you and I are connected by magic?" I guess I'm bolder when I wake up rested than when I'm

64

tired. I've avoided this conversation for a while, and I'm still not ready to face what I think is happening between the savage and me, but I asked the question, and I can't take it back. Preparing for the answer as if it's gonna hit me like a brick on the forehead, I brace.

"Yes."

Swallowing, I nod.

"It is nighttime." He finally answers my first question and starts braiding the long charcoal strands of his hair while I pull my knees up and watch him. After a while, he pauses and extends a hand. "Come."

I shake my head.

"You smell worse than Brokko. Come."

Scoffing, I shake my head. But he's right. My smell isn't worse than Brokko, but it's pretty bad. I haven't bathed since the evening of the savages' attack when Tolei bathed me. This brings up images of his hands rubbing my body, and my skin starts tingling. I ignore the sensation. "It sure feels like an entire moon," I say.

"What does?" he asks in a low baritone voice that only makes my skin tingle more, my body heating up along with it.

"Come," he repeats, and this time, it's an order. "I want to pet you."

"I just want to wash up."

"We'll do that too. Come." He chuckles with a big smile.

"What's funny?"

"I keep repeating myself. If you were one of my males, I would have strapped you to a tree and left you behind so you could take some time to think about your behavior. Spending time alone and abandoned tends to bring clarity of thought and a will to correct one's actions."

Damn. "You sound like a king or something."

"I'm an Alpha or nothing."

Double damn.

"Come," he repeats himself and laughs.

Reluctantly, I toss back the covers. Holy fuck, it's cold. I rush to the pond and jump in. Hot hot hot! "Fuuuuuk. Me." I huff and puff, trapped in a hot bath, neither wanting to get out nor wanting to stay in.

Wide-eyed, Tolei stares.

Luckily, my body adjusts, and I lean back, mimicking his pose. "I'm good, I'm good. Top of the morning to you too."

He blinks. "That seemed eventful for you."

I laugh. "No tea is why. Can't think clearly without tea."

"Your tea is in the sack."

He brought my tea. Awww. I hate that he brought my tea. I love that he brought my tea. I wouldn't have brought anything, and look where it would get me, having nothing in the middle of a cave. "Thank you," I say.

"Welcome," he purrs. In his eyes, the gold swivels with the red and replaces it. Tolei's gaze roams my body, and I make a conscious effort against covering up. I'm not ashamed of my body, but facing a male built as perfectly as one of the goddess's lovers makes me more self-conscious than on most days.

I'm a bit overweight, with a few rolls that show my love for indulging in fatty foods. I'm also in my late thirties, and certain parts of my body have loosened with age. Like my tits. They used to be perkier. They're not sagging, they're just not as perky as they were when I was eighteen. My thighs, though, they take on all the meals and don't let go.

"What feels like an entire moon?" Tolei asks.

"I have no idea."

"You said it felt like an entire moon."

"Did I?" I dunk under the water, then emerge and huff out a breath. "Did you bring my soap?"

Tolei leaps out of the pond, splashing water everywhere. He walks to my sack, and I get an eyeful of his naked body, specifically his strong legs and an ass I could break my nails off on when I try to squeeze it. Hot damn.

When he bends to find the soap inside my bag, his sac and cock hang heavy and large between his legs. My body lights up like an inferno.

Because I'm too busy gawking at him, I don't see the moment Tolei pitches the bar of soap at me. I yelp, arms out, trying to catch it, but the soap slips through my fingers, hits my chest, and falls into the water. I dive for it. Eyes open underwater, I'm scrambling to catch the damn thing, but it keeps slipping from my grip. With both hands, I'm working on the stupid soap, regretting I ever asked for it while trying not to drown (again) at the bottom of a pond. There! I grip it tightly, dig my fingernails into it, and catapult out of the water with the soap in my hand. "I got it!"

Tolei's eyes are as wide as they can be.

"Got the soap." I show him the soap.

"Congratulations," he says, but mutters something in his own language while slipping back into the water. "My mistake. It has been...no. It has never been that I have had to spend time with a king's female."

"Hmm. Does that mean you've spent time with a non-king female?"

Tolei smirks. "I am too old not to have spent time with a female."

My ears are burning. I wish I'd never asked him anything.

"You smell a little angry," he says. "Are you jealous?"

I want to hit him over the head with the soap. "I am not. It was just a question."

"It was a very specific question having very little to do with the point I was making. Are you sure you want to keep asking questions like these? Or shall we continue with our pleasant and eventful evening talking about soap and tea."

Unsure why I give a shit or why I asked about the females, I shrug. Sometimes, I wish he wasn't so forward or so perceptive or that he would evade a little more than he does. But I doubt that'll ever happen. It's something I'll have to live with. Or not live with, because I plan to escape his clutches eventually. Just not tonight.

"I expected you to catch the soap effortlessly," Tolei says.

"You pitched it like you attended diamond cross games." I mimic the pitcher at the cross game by pulling my elbow back and tossing the soap at the savage male. He doesn't even look at it, but catches it instantly. I bet this male could catch a fly with his bare fist. And probably eat it.

"Do you eat flies?" I ask.

"I could, yes."

"Ew."

"What's *ew* about it?" He pushes off his end of the pond and starts walking toward me.

Oh no. I eye the exit, then his muscles. Exit, muscles, exit, muscles, strong hands that will wash my body and scrub and rub... Okay, I'll stay.

The savage offers me the soap, eyes molten gold.

"Didn't dare throw the soap again," he says, voice low, rough, seductive.

I take the soap, and he retreats to his former position.

Disappointed that he didn't wash me, I shrug as if I don't care and start washing my hair first. It's so caked up with dirt that I'm a bit embarrassed I haven't bathed for so long. Actually, I shouldn't be embarrassed. The horde pillaged my village and took me prisoner. It's not as if I could have demanded a bath or even this bar of soap. He should be ashamed of how he treated a woman. With that thought, I jut out my jaw and proceed to clean up thoroughly, washing my hair three times and my body twice.

"Are you finished?" he asks.

I nod, and when he extends his hand, I figure he's waiting for the bar of soap so he can wash. What is wrong with me? The guy just wants to be clean, and I'm the one who's having all the dirty thoughts about his muscles and the sac between his legs.

"I didn't realize you are waiting to wash as well. Here." I place the soap in his palm.

He puts it back into mine. "Keep it."

Okay. Awkward.

Tolei throws back his head. Looking at the ceiling, he rises to his full height, letting his claws scrape the stone on the ground like knives. They leave marks, deep white grooves carved into the stone forever. "Wash me."

Damn. I hesitate. Last time I touched him, my body heated up from the inside out. Tolei can turn me into an insatiable little slut in want of his cock. The magic spells me and draws me under its power. Even if I wanted to, I can't resist.

He sighs and, in an almost bored voice, repeats, "Come. Wash me."

"I heard you the first time."

"Good. Now heed the words that are coming out of my mouth."

"I'm not touching you, savage."

Tolei pins me with a gaze. "Call me savage again, and I will show you how savage I can be."

I don't know why I goad him. Maybe a part of me likes to test him. Maybe I'm insane for this male shouldn't be pushed, and we're alone and he could hurt me anytime he wants. Or maybe he really is mine, and I can feel it on some weird magical level I can't grasp. Maybe his mating story is true. "Savage," I say.

Oh, I regret saying that.

In a tick, he's at me, and I don't even have time to scream before he spins me around, bends me over, and fists my hair. He yanks my hair so my back flexes, jutting out my chest. His mouth touches the side of my neck, the most vulnerable part of the body. I wonder if this is my end. I wonder if he'll bite down and rip out a chunk of me.

Moments pass as he growls low in his throat, his breaths huffing over my pulse.

Tolei presses his front to my back. His erection rests heavily on my behind, heating me up so much, the pond suddenly feels cold. I stare at the ice on the ceiling that's reflecting us in the water below.

He towers behind me with his head at my neck, sniffing over my shoulder while his huge clawed hand with those long thick fingers comes around and lands on my belly. He presses against my belly, and his cock pulses. The male starts purring at my ear, whispering something in a language I don't understand, and my body responds.

The tingling sensation spreads all over my skin, raising goose bumps along the way to my nipples, which harden. My breasts become heavy and need sucking and touching and molding, and only this male can give that to me. My clit starts throbbing as if it's being stroked, but he's not touching me. He's whispering and purring, and I swear it's like his mouth is over my clit, licking it, stroking it, making me want to come. Pain zaps my lower belly, and he pushes against it with his palm. Liquid leaks out of my pussy.

I gasp at the sensation.

It's not quite an orgasm, but it's something that releases the pressure inside my channel and makes my pussy throb for the real thing.

His cock pulses again, and he spins me around, towering over me, eyes molten gold, black pupils tiny inside them. Tolei bends and presses his lips to mine.

I don't resist. He's warm and hard, and I need him.

He kisses the corner of my mouth, my nose, cheeks, then just stands there watching me. The purr intensifies as he takes my hand and presses it over his chest so I can feel the vibrations.

"Open your mouth and welcome my kiss."

As if on command, I can feel my heartbeat in my clit. Holy Lord, what the hell is going on here? Tolei doesn't wait for me to open my mouth. His tongue swoops into my mouth the way he swooped into my village: sudden, uninvited, and with the heat of a thousand suns. The purring grows in volume as he presses me against him, one broad palm at the small of my back so that my breasts feel the vibrations.

I throw my arms around his neck.

The second I do, the palm at the small of my back travels to my behind. He squeezes and moans again, adding his second hand to hold me up. I wrap my legs around his waist, and we make out like two youngsters at the village fair.

When he stops and leaves the pond, I want him back.

CHAPTER
ELEVEN

TOLEI

My people say that the sigil never lies, that one of my kind can never mistake his mate, but after the king drained the last female of my kind, I lost hope I'd ever mate. I even forgot about the existence of the massive sigil on my chest, the one that holds powerful magic I have no access to until Andy gives it to me.

It shines bright gold now, pulsing on my chest. An inconvenience since the king can detect our magic and the sigil acts as a beacon for my enemies. Therefore, I must mask it, and it pains me to have to do so. I would like nothing more than to roam the lands as free as a bird in the sky, proudly bare-chested with a big shiny sigil telling everyone who dares to look that I have, indeed, mated a female.

Perhaps, one span, when the king is gone and forgotten, I shall again roam free, but not alone, and that is the span I am prepared to die for tonight.

"Where are you going?" my mate asks, her lips swollen and as red as her cheeks. I can't tell if she's hot or embarrassed, perhaps a bit of both. I know that her people consider us savages, animals with whom they won't mate, and even though I would have enjoyed exhibiting the savage ways of fucking her, it is not time. She's not ready for mounting. I went easy on her, though I would have liked nothing more than to plunder her little pussy.

Andy leaves the pond and stands next to me as I grab some clothes from my sack. A black leather kilt. That'll do. I strap on my daggers, the big ax, the baby ax I made when some asshole broke the handle of my other big ax. I eye my spare knives, contemplate leaving them to Andy. She seems to like them and would use them. I'll leave those for her.

I pull my hair in a messy knot at the back of my head, leaving her braid, the one I cut off her head and pinned to my scalp, falling over my shoulder.

"That's my hair, isn't it?"

I nod and cross my arms over my chest, assuming a battle stance because she's gonna berate me about giving her a haircut. Andy approaches, completely nude, her breasts swaying.

Licking my teeth, I purr, imagining those big breasts even bigger and full of milk for my baby.

Andy likes the purr. It's cute how it makes her horny, and I'm certain she has no idea that when she's outside the water, I can scent her arousal as well as the way her body responds to my proximity. She emits her own mating scent that tells me how she feels, not to mention the sigil on my chest pulses, telling me of my mate's need. "Your pussy is leaking, isn't it? Coating your channel for ease of entry."

"No." Andy runs her fingers over her braid where it rests over my shoulder. "It looks strange seeing it on you."

"It looks better on me."

She chuckles. "There's something deranged about you cutting my braid and attaching it to your head."

"Better your hair than your head, no?"

"Oh, Tolei, you are not allowed in society at all."

I laugh. "Savage is as savage does."

She traces the sigil that's pulsing on my chest, and the scent her pussy emits calls me. I can almost hear her pussy begging. *Please, savage king, plunder me, plunder me.*

I find her clawless fingers, lack of prominent muscular structure, and small feminine features attractive and cute, and I wanna fuck her so bad, my balls might explode. They're full of seed and weigh heavy between my legs, even bothering me when I'm walking.

She bites her lip, rises on her toes, and sniffs my chest. "You smell."

I sniff, nostrils flaring. "I smell good."

"Yes," she whispers as if someone will hear us. The horse, no doubt, can hear us, but most of us have developed one form of acoustic shielding technique or another over the long turns of our lives.

The world the goddess created us in changed, became more noisy. It didn't use to be this way. No carriages, no weapons, no chatter. Only the horde roaming the lands, hunting, drinking, eating. Then Stenants came, followed by fae and others, and it became less about enjoying life and more about survival of the fittest. Since my people were the fittest, the others banded together to steal our magic and eventually destroy us. Not all of us, though, as I'm about to show Andy's king.

Thoughts of the king deflate my dick. I step back and continue dressing.

"Are you going somewhere?" she asks.

I nod.

"Where?"

"Wherever I please."

"Then I shall apply the same freedoms to myself."

I point at the furs. "You will stay here."

"We already went over this, Tolei. I'm not your pet."

"You are my mate, and you will stay safe."

"From what?"

My ears twitch as I stretch my hearing outside our small space and into the main cave, where males are bitching me out because of my lateness.

"Is there danger I'm not aware of?" she asks.

Our plan to attack the king's position isn't information I'm going to share with her tonight. I trust her very little with this information, and my males' lives are at stake. I walk forward so she has to walk back or fall. She trips over the fur, and I grab her, then gently lay her down on the plush bedding. I kiss her nose. "Stay in the cave. I will return bloody, and the blood won't be mine. Spilling your people's blood makes me horny. I will want to fuck. Hard. Think about how hard I'll fuck you while covered in the blood of those who wronged me. Revenge shall be served warm, in the form of their flesh stuck between my teeth."

Andy presses a hand over her mouth. "That's terrible."

"Your king is terrible. Now we're back, and we're gonna consume everything on our way to him."

"Some of those people are innocent," she says.

"Most of my people were too. The king didn't care, so neither shall I."

The moment I step outside the privacy our little area provides, Kasei appears before me, making me think he was listening to my private conversations the entire time. He was. I know he was. Damn him. I grab his throat, digging my claws into it. "What are you doing here, Kasei?"

His eyes glow red, his magic resisting mine. I dislike the dominance I sense from him and squeeze tighter, noting

I'm more aggressive with him than usual. Kasei jabs his claws into my side, and I snarl, throwing him down the tunnel, advancing on him. When I grab him again, he turns up his head, giving me clear access to his throat, a sign of trust and submission.

Drawing back my upper lip, I growl a warning as I sniff the soft place where his neck meets his shoulder. Satisfied that Kasei let me get this close to his jugular and that his magic has retreated, I step back and hold my side. My hands come away bloody, the sigil that makes me heal fast glowing, draining my magic.

"What the hell is going on with you two?" Neensei asks, my horde lined up with him by the cave's exit.

"There's nothing wrong with me," I announce.

"Oh, I beg to differ," Mag mutters as she brushes past me.

Kasei growls at her. "Where are you going?"

She doesn't answer him, and before he runs off chasing pussy the same way I might've if it were Andy, I throw an arm over his shoulder and lead him toward the exit. "I have a mate, and I want to enjoy her. What the hell are you doing sneaking around my home?" The cave is a home to me for as long as I stay there.

"The mating sigil is made so the female manipulates you. What if she uses it to the king's advantage?"

"She knows nothing of how the sigil works."

"The king uses tricks. Maybe she's not yours."

I grab his cheeks, barely holding myself back from twisting his neck. "Never say she's not mine again." I release him, but I know Kasei won't stop questioning my mating bond. I have no time to deal with him now. I have to lead the horde to the king's position. We're running late already.

"I'm looking out for us all, Alpha."

Pushing past him and my horde, I exit the cave and start scaling the mountain. For the first time in centuries, I wonder if some of them will choose not to follow me. Soon, however, I hear claws scraping the stone and know my horde is following, but if Kasei keeps this up, some will change their minds, might even think they could replace me. Kasei has to leave my horde.

Neensei catches up with me, his blond braid wrapped tightly around his neck as a form of armor. "Hey, Alpha?"

"Hey," I grunt out as my foot slips, and I find a better position for it, pushing up as I scale the steep incline.

"The older pet is very cute," he says.

"She's not a pet." I'm a hypocrite. "And Kasei claimed her."

"She's not his mate."

I frown. "You don't want to fight him for her, do you?"

"Maybe. Would you mind?"

"Not if you win."

I'm telling him Kasei should leave the horde or get himself eliminated from the horde. Kasei sniffing near my mate's sister is one thing. Sniffing near my mate is something else entirely.

"Who stayed behind?" I ask.

"Nobody."

"Someone has to stay behind."

"The pets can't escape us, Alpha."

I pause and stare at him, and he looks at me like I'm stupid. He's stupid. "Sure they can. They have legs. Didn't you see how my mate ran? She's fast and swims well." He seems confused. "Do you disagree?"

"She runs super well and super fast, Alpha."

"That's right." We keep climbing, but Neensei keeps

glancing at me as he climbs, and I'm afraid if I don't ask what it is he wants to say, he'll pay more attention to whatever is on his mind than to the mountain we're ascending, which could result in a fall and injury. The seventeen males in my horde are all of what's left of what once numbered close to seven hundred.

"Spit it out," I order.

"Why would anyone stay behind?"

"To protect the females."

"Won't the mating sigil protect the females?"

It would if my mate accepted the mating. If she accepts her end of the mating bond, I could protect her no matter my location. The sigil binds us, and even separated, she could call me, and I would appear near her in an instant. I am her beast, created for her protection. The horde knows how mating works, and now they also know I have not mated her. In the horde, respect of one's charges is second only to the strength of any one Alpha. Leaders should be both feared and respected.

Her refusal reflects poorly on me and might even encourage Kasei's ambition to take over my horde.

I look behind me. Red eyes blink in the darkness, and behind them, the small cave entrance is almost invisible. Leaving Andy makes me uneasy, but she's safe there, and besides, my horse is hungry and would consume any intruder at this stage of his hunger. I keep him hungry so that when we raid, he is more eager to kill.

"Everyone was under the impression you already mated, Alpha." Neensei pats my shoulder. "You'll get laid soon. I have faith in you."

Oh, fuck me. "Thank you, Neensei."

"Anytime, Alpha. It was nice chatting with you. Maybe we can chat more often."

"We shall never speak of this again."

"Right. Off I go." He pauses and wiggles his ass, assuring the firmness of the rock before leaping up and sprint climbing toward the top, his agile muscles straining to keep up with the change into a quicker pace. My males rush past me, and soon I realize what they've done. Neensei chatted me up so they could all race past their Alpha and make it there before I did.

"Little cunts," I hiss.

Snickering ensues, and I pick up the pace, racing them to the king's position near the top.

~

ANDY

RIGHT AS TOLEI LEAVES, MAG ENTERS THROUGH THE TUNNEL, HER steps urgent, waking the horse from his nap. He snorts at her and makes his way out of the cave. Mag stops abruptly, takes account of me in the furs, and I instantly feel bad for being clean while she's still in tattered clothes with red marks on her ankles from those awful shackles.

My face heats up. I'm taking comfort in the savage's furs and his touch while my sister needs care.

Mag rests her fists on her hips. "Okay, so I was coming here to see if this would be a grand time to escape seeing as we've been left alone, but now I'm standing here thinking I'd like to bathe in that nice steaming pond, maybe get you to take out the knots from my hair, and tell me why you have a glint in your eyes." Mag descends and stops at the bath while I leave the furs in search of fresh soap for her.

Tolei carries a large sack, a few smaller ones, and a

wooden chest that's locked. I check a small sack for soap first and find stones, random branches, dry herbs that remind me of the supplies Mag and I had in our healing cabinet. Is he also a healer?

"What are you looking for?" Mag asks and I hear the water splash before she sighs. It pleases me Mag is here. I can't imagine my life without Mag, and I am both sad and happy Tolei took my sister along with me. Sad because she has to endure the captivity, happy because we're in it together.

"I'm looking for fresh soap." I keep searching, digging into another small sack, this one made of soft brown suede.

"Tolei." She says his name as if she likes saying it. It's coming off all wrong from her lips and making me upset.

Pausing, I turn to see that Mag's resting her head over the edge of the pond, a blissful expression on her face. Her eyes are closed.

"Savage," I correct her, practically barking it.

"Is that your pet name for him?"

"It's not a pet name," I say, getting defensive, several layers of guilt eating at me. One, I let him touch me, and two, I'm jealous of my own sister saying his name in that sexy way Mag says things with her musical fairylike voice.

Mag smiles. "I'm messing with you, Andy."

"I know."

"You should also know better than to think I will judge what you do or who you do it with."

Now I feel even guiltier because Mag is perfect, and I'm blessed that she's my sister. I peek inside the suede sack and find a decorative lamp, tiny bottles of oils, several pretty combs, rings, necklaces, bracelets, pendants. All gold, and some with clear, shiny precious stones. "Holy crap, it's a treasure sack." Gold mine! I grab the sack and sit by the pond, where I open it in my lap.

"Oh no, oh no," Mag says, faking shock in her best pompous girl-from-Lyan-city accent, "my virgin eyes have seen your breasts."

"My fair lady," I say in the same accent. "I am poor and have no clothes to cover my breasts with."

"Awww, I shall then spend my riches on you. Take what you will from the..." Mag pauses and swims over. "Fuck, that's fine-combed suede." She runs a wet palm over the sack.

"Stay in character," I tell her.

Mag nods. "I shall shower you with riches. Whatever you find in my humble abode"—she makes a grand gesture by sweeping her thin arm to encompass the cave—"you may keep. Besides the savage's dick. I see you've already kept that one."

I punch her in the shoulder.

Mag dunks under the water, stands back up with a smile. "Well, how big is it?"

Unwilling to talk about Tolei's dick (it's the biggest dick in the land I'm pretty sure if it), I walk back to the sacks in search of soap and clothes and find only a few pairs of pants. I wrap a soft fur around my body and grab one for my sister after the bath.

Returning, I sit with her by the pond. Mag turns her back to me and I grab the beautiful comb from Tolei's sack and comb her hair while she watches the water.

"You will stay with him," she says.

"He's keeping me inside a cave. I don't have much choice."

"If you did, would you leave?"

I pause the combing. "I'd go anywhere with you, Mag. You know that."

"It's the middle of the night. We're inside Mount Havensi, which has an active wild animal population."

"And raiders."

"And rebels."

"And horde."

Mag chuckles. "Raiders, rebels, and animals will run from the horde."

I laugh. "Everyone runs except us. What's that say about us?"

"That we're crazy," my sister concludes as she snatches the suede sack. She takes out a necklace with a green teardrop emerald and places it on my lap.

"Do you think your savage would mind if we wore some of this looted jewelry?"

I don't miss her use of *your*. "I don't know him well enough to say."

"I don't either, but I have a feeling these are yours anyway."

I think Mag is right. Tolei didn't go through all the trouble of bringing me with him just for sex. With his looks, he could have just about any girl. The mating thing might actually be real, and if that's so, I need to know what it means.

I snap the necklace around Mag's slender neck. The emerald matches her eyes, and pretty shiny things bring a smile to my sister's face. She's so part fairy, I swear it.

W e lie in wait, observing the magic detector, a blue beacon of light situated on a pole erected above the small cave entrance near the top of the mountain. We came to neutralize the detector so we can cross the mountain range undetected while I set up wards around our camp. Wards require the use of specialized sigils that emit magical signatures I believe the beacons can pick up on.

The king wouldn't expect us to risk scaling Mount Havensi only to raid this small, nearly defenseless location. There's no gold or riches here, only a stupid blinking light, but the king considers us animals who raid for food and shelter, so he wouldn't know what we'd want in the first place.

For one, he suspects we wouldn't notice the clever use of Stenan beacons as magic detectors. And that we wouldn't pay attention to the glowing lights at the top of his flagpoles all around the land. Would have ignored it had it not been for that one soldier back a moon ago who stabbed me in the thigh with the flagpole. The sharp end of the pole pierced my flesh, and when he jabbed me harder, the beacon entered my muscle along with the entire tip of the pole.

I got the pole out of my thigh right after I ripped the soldier's heart out of his rib cage. After the battle, I tended to my wounds and dug out a broken blue beacon. It reeked of magic that wasn't mine and made my wound fester for spans.

It was then I decided not to raid with the horde, but to remain outside the villages and towns, watching the raid from the highest nearby point. The blue beacons kept appearing, and any use of our magic made them light up red instead of blue. We stopped using sigils when I figured out these beacons were connected and they were sending information back to the king, who then deployed soldiers to our location. Or worse, medeisars.

The soldier who gave up the location of this beacon surrendered right after Neensei ripped his gut open, so the information about the post being unguarded is questionable.

The entrance to the cave appears crafted instead of a naturally formed part of the mountain. This tells me men made it. It's a small opening, however, barely large enough for an adult male to pass through. It would be rather uncomfortable and stupid for soldiers to have to squeeze in and out of their posts. Naturally, this strange opening worries me. I don't like things I don't know, and there's so much about this new world I don't know. However, I'll learn as I encounter the strangeness, beacons and inefficient little entries included.

Either way, something's here along with the beacon, and we intend to check it out. If the king's post is full of his males, we'll kill the soldiers and neutralize the beacon. But there's more here than a beacon and a few males. Warmth is spreading over my skin, wanting to mingle with my sigils. It is another's magic inviting mine for a dance.

We've lain in wait for a long while now, and the horde awaits my orders while we practically hang from the steep mountain holding on to the rocks by the sheer force of our endurance. My muscles are starting to twitch from exhaustion, and I can either progress up the mountain and kill the beacon or fall off and die.

I don't have time for dying right now, so I invite the warm magic for a dance. It slithers over my skin, seeking a sigil to connect with, and stops at my chest. Like a curious child, it pokes it, a lighthearted probe near my sternum. The sigil isn't mine, so it doesn't respond, and the magic moves on and over my shoulder, traveling upward.

This magic is old. Familiar. Innocent.

While the magic probes me, I make a move toward the beacon, and the horde follows.

Wait a moment.

We're stealthy, but not this stealthy. I hear nothing, not even my males' breathing. It's as if we're in a vacuum. Next to me, Kasei narrows his eyes. I tilt my head, silently telling him to listen. He shakes his head.

I scrape my claw over a rock.

No sound.

Fuck, something's wrong here. It's too quiet. We climbed thousands of clicks up the mountain with no one noticing. It was all too easy. While the king's people are our prey, they're far from helpless or stupid, and I have a bad feeling.

Sticking two fingers into my mouth, I whistle.

Kasei doesn't move, and neither do any of my males.

He's staring at me.

I blow into my fingers, a long loud whistle.

When he can't hear me, I balance on the rock with one arm and dangle from the mountain so I can get the horn unhooked from my belt. I blow it, and Kasei's eyes widen. He starts shouting and crawling back down, but it's too late. Nets land on his body, and heavy chains that weigh him down. Kasei's claws scrape the mountainside as he hangs on for dear life. Some of the males note what's happening and move toward our position, but the majority of the horde is focused on the beacon. When hunting, we communicate by sound, not sight, and now we're in some sort of sound vacuum.

The ground above starts shaking as if people are stomping on it.

Soldiers in red uniforms crawl out of the small entrance like snakes and rush toward us.

We're hanging ducks.

I check the beacon.

It's still blinking blue, meaning my choice not to use magic is correct.

A heavy net drops on my head, and I lose balance, stumbling down and cutting my belly. The pain makes me scream, the wound deep and burning. I catch myself on the net the soldiers threw to capture me and wrap myself in it. They're pulling Kasei upward, along with at least seven other horde males. I'm not leaving my males here. I would rather get captured with my horde than be the one to return home without seven males. That's almost half of my horde, and I can't afford to lose that many males. Or any males.

Inside the net, I stop struggling and check my gut wound. I think my intestines might spill. Eh. No time to worry about small things right now. I don't intend to die.

Emerging onto the clearing before the cave entrance, I

catch sight of several males in red uniforms operating a machine that seems to have emerged out of the mountain. It's a large spinning wheel to which the chains from the nets are attached, and as the wheel spins, the chains draw the nets toward it.

Kasei reaches the wheel first, and a king's miner in a blue robe emerges and brings a tiny pipe to his mouth. He blows on it. Out flies a single dart, but just before it hits Kasei, it disperses into golden dust. Magic slides over my skin, the old innocent one. It invites my healing sigil to dance. I don't answer it and struggle to contain my magic with all my might lest I trip the blinking blue beacon and fail the mission. The miner passes the darts to the soldiers and they keep blowing them at us.

The cries of my males as the magic attacks them are muted because the fucking miner is an Acoustico, a man who wields sound-tampering magic. In pain and unwilling to use their magic, my males are struggling to hold their position while I'm stuck under the metal net, trapped, held tightly and unable to move.

The beacon blinks blue, and I have to choose. Alert the king of our exact position by using my magic and triggering the beacon, or lose some of my males. The choice is easy. I deploy my magic.

Three battle sigils ignite an angry red and rip off my skin, then start spinning all around me as I rise and growl at the miner.

I flick my wrists, and the sigils slice the chains.

Turning, I flick my wrist, and a sigil cuts the machine and returns to spin with the other two around me. Swords drawn, the soldiers attack, and I roar and deploy the sigils to slice them up into tiny fucking pieces.

On my way to the cave, I stomp over one man's eye, squashing it with my boot.

Inside the cave, I seek the runaway miner, but find the innocent old magic, begging me to dance.

Entering a small dark alcove, I inhale and recognize the scent. A pair of red eyes blink inside the cave. Huddled in the corner of the cave is a medium-sized medeisar, a magical creature the king's miners trapped and are mining for magic. This one, looking pathetic and crazy, still has patches of soft pale brown fur, telling me his age. Under twenty turns for sure, which tells me the king might have medeisar females he's breeding in captivity. The medeisars I would expect to encounter as I raid should be older than this boy, somewhere around my age.

Even young, a medeisar is a beast, and, when standing on all fours, he comes up past my waistline. Saliva drips from his mouth, and he growls at me, showing me his pointy canines, claws extended, tail tucked under. He will attack. The only reason he hasn't yet is because my magic confuses him.

I'm not his Alpha, but my sigils never lie. My magic is felt by all the savages, crazy creatures included. The creature smells of the king's rotten magic, but somewhere inside the boy, there's still magic that recognizes mine. It wants to dance, to submit, to let me comfort him. If I don't have to, I will not kill the creature.

But I know better than that.

Despite the three sigils circling me, the medeisar lunges. Only knowing a hunger for flesh, even if it's their own flesh they're hunting, medeisars are killing machines, the king's most powerful weapons, those he used to destroy the hordes.

I deploy the sigils and turn away, for once grateful that

the miner in charge of this post is an Acoustico and I can't hear the carnage as my sigils dice the creature up into pieces to ensure it's truly dead. Medeisars are hard to kill, almost impossible.

With the death of the medeisar from which the miner channeled magic and made the area silent, sound returns outside. A flash of blue robe escapes through a blinding green light that disappears as fast as it appeared. A hidden portal. Borrowed fae magic. The damn miner is gone.

That's fine. We shall meet in Lyan, where I will take great pleasure in cutting off and then wearing his ears as pendants from the necklace I'll make out of his intestines.

Happy thoughts make me smile as the three sigils return and embed themselves in my skin.

My horde is releasing the captured males. I count seventeen. Still in the net, Kasei is immobile, but breathing on his own.

When I see one of my males has taken the beacon we came here to disarm, not to ignite or steal, I blow into my horn, and my males prepare to descend back down the mountain. I grab the net and yank it off Kasei's unmoving body. Picking him up, I throw him over my shoulder and secure him with one arm and carefully start my descent so I don't drop him and kill both of us in the process.

CARRYING KASEI DOWN THE MOUNTAIN TAKES A TOLL ON MY BODY, and by the time I return to the cave, the horde is waiting for me. After the beacon turned red, I used my healing sigil on Kasei because his heart stopped beating twice on the way down.

I drop him at the entrance and kneel, beaten and depleted, my head spinning from blood loss.

When we use sigils, they deplete us of magic, and we have to replenish ourselves if we want to reuse them. We replenish ourselves the same way the king's people rejuvenate their energy, with food, water, and rest. I need all three tonight, but will take rest and water only and save the food for some other night after I've left this place.

"The beacon?"

Neensei throws it, and I catch the pulsing red ball in my hand and weigh it. This way of channeling magic is similar to the way we use sigils to direct our magic, but the magic I have is mine. The magic the king and his miners wield is stolen and destroys the source until nothing's left of it. The medeisar, who would've been a normal healthy male, was used and abused, kept in the dark, trapped in madness until I killed him.

Whispers of his gentle, innocent magic still remain on my skin. They'll be gone soon, and nobody will ever know what happened to him. Has the boy ever even had anyone? The king will pay for this.

Neensei presses a hand over the gaping wound on my belly. I stare at his hand, then up at him.

A smile appears on his face. "Just want to be sure you don't trip over your guts when they fall out."

"Thank you."

"Anytime, Alpha. You want me to heal you?"

The red beacon pulses, and I want to test my new sigil against it. Since I speculated that the king has found a way to detect magical sources and these beacons communicate with him, I grab a dagger and carve a new sigil onto my calf, one I believe will make my magic untraceable. With a thought, I ignite the new sigil and rejoice when it wraps around the beacon. The beacon turns blue.

The horde cheers. We are no longer detectable. We can

now sneak right up to the gates of Lyan and destroy it with every single sigil at our disposal before the king even knows magic is at play.

A moment later, the beacon turns red.

"Fuck." I crush the damn thing in my hand, glass shattering, pieces of it cutting my palm.

My healing sigil starts to glow. It's faint, but will heal my wounds.

I assess the males. They look beat. After scaling the mountain and not eating for several spans, we'll need a long stretch of rest to recuperate. And it's not just the physical beating they took up there, there's also the blow to morale. The sigil I carved was supposed to work and mask the beacon so we can use our magic and roam the lands undetected. We don't fear the king, but we're not stupid either. Seventeen of us. Seven hundred thousand of his soldiers. I would have to be stupid not to account for our odds and use what tools I have to avoid the conflict until I'm united with my brothers and their males.

"We are the Kilseleian horde."

The males nod.

"We have roamed the lands before the king did, or any of his people, no matter how old. We roamed, we raided, and we took whatever we wanted whenever we wanted. We shall survive the king and many more like him."

The horde hoots.

"Pack. Be ready to move. We do not stop until we reach Lyan."

Groaning ensues, the males mumble under their breaths. I hear words like "beat" and "sore."

"What?" I tap my ear. "Was that whining? Oh, I'm sorry we had a tiny setback. I'm sorry some of you are tired. Would you like me to make you tea? Bunch of horde males sitting at the cave's entrance greeting the sun with a cup of tea. Like little fairy fuckers and their morning routines."

The males snicker.

"We keep moving, and we do not stop until we or the king are dead. Clear?"

"Yes, Alpha!"

I enter the cave. Neensei steps in my way, both hands on my shoulders. "Your intestines are now hanging outside your belly."

I look down. Why, yes they are. I push my guts inside and deploy the healing sigil. It seals the wound, but makes me sway on my feet. Healing magic exhausts me because the nurturing magic isn't my primary magic. If I'm using a sigil that's not a battle sigil, I have to expend twice as much effort as I would if I'd deployed ten sigils that could destroy an entire village and all the king's people in it. But the horde has no healer, for healing magic is mostly developed by females, and we make do with what we have.

Our journey is getting harder and harder the closer we get to the Lyan. When we awoke and set out for the capital, we had the element of surprise, but with the growing refugees moving north and into Lyan, rumors of our conquests have spread.

At the end of the tunnel, I stop and lean against the cave's cold wall. There are not one but two females in my furs.

Okay, maybe my night isn't turning out so bad after all.

"Neensei?"

His footsteps approach from behind. "We're not packed yet, but soon. Oh," he says as he sees the females in the furs. I smell his arousal. "It would be a shame to wake the females now."

"I agree."

"You do?"

I nod.

"We leave at dawn instead of now?" he asks in a hopeful tone.

"Neensei, for as long as I breathe and lead this horde, tiredness is an invalid excuse."

"We rested when the females got tired."

I blink. "Do you have a pussy?"

"Nah, but sometimes I want one."

My eyes widen, and Neensei belly laughs and points at me. "The look on your face. Priceless. I'm joking."

"I don't think you are. I think you want a pussy."

"I want one on my face." He licks his lips.

Sighing, I wave him off. "Go and wake the blonde and travel with her."

That shuts him up. He rubs the back of his neck. "Kasei won't like that."

"I know." It will provoke Kasei to make his move, and I'll deal with him then. The horde can't afford divisions, and Kasei would make his case for leadership at a time when our enemy is everywhere and everyone in the land wants to kill us. An Alpha protects his horde, and sometimes that means eliminating the threats within.

THIRTEEN

TOLEI

We traveled for another two spans before the males started sleepwalking, their knees folding, strength giving out while I scouted ahead for potential threats. The Acoustico miner up on that mountain used a portal to escape. Portals are fae magic, and I have to presume the fae alliances with the king are alive and well as they were back when they banded together and destroyed my people.

I made Kasei set up my tent and comb the furs my mate's resting on with her sister. He hated that and left the tent huffing and puffing. Good. After recovering from his wounds, he behaved like an entitled little shit and needed a lesson in humility.

There's only one female in the bed now, the older one sitting beside her, holding vigil over the younger one.

"I have a brother like you," I say as I sharpen my ax. Spitting on the blade for better traction, I move the sharpener over the edge, imagining the moment when I enter the gates of Lyan and this very blade slices through the king's people. Happy thoughts.

The female isn't responding, and I feel like chatting

with her. She is pleasant, but reminds me too much of the fae folk, whom I dislike almost as much as the king's people.

"My older brother used to watch over me," I continue when she remains quiet. "And my other siblings."

"Oh." The female glances down, then quickly back up. I think my mate, who is lying on her side and facing her sister, is awake and pretending to sleep while I speak with her sister. Just as well.

"How many siblings do you have?" the sister asks.

"Two now. I had twenty-seven."

Her eyes widen. "Twenty-seven and now two."

An understanding passes through her eyes, and her face drops, her gaze on my mate.

"They're dead," I say.

"I'm sorry to hear that."

"No, you're not."

"I am too."

I snort and set my ax and the sharpener to the side, then take the little dart Neensei picked up from the dead soldier. It's full of iron-laced magic. Since it's cracked, it leaks iron. "Ever seen one of these?" I toss it at her, and she catches it and examines it while iron leaks between her fingers. She isn't bothered by it, so she's either not a fae or too mixed with the king's blood for iron to bother her.

The sister hands me back the item. "Never seen it before. What is it?"

"Iron darts." The king once used liquid iron to threaten the fae, but has since upgraded his weapons and now uses darts laced with magic to disperse iron. The iron itself slows us down a bit, but it won't hurt us the way it would a fae. But these darts with iron-laced magic worry me. They knocked down my males.

"I have a favor to ask of you," I say.

Her green eyes positively shine with fae glee. "Are you bargaining with me, savage?"

I chuckle. "A vial of your blood in exchange for..." I pause for effect as I pull out a tiny sack holding a piece of jewelry I stole from the fae prince. I dangle the sack in front of her.

Green fairy eyes twinkle at the prospect of seeing what's inside.

I toss it to her, and she catches it, but doesn't peek inside as I expected her to. "What do you need a vial of my blood for?"

"I will show my healing sigil how it can be resistant to the iron and magic mix the king is using."

"I'm resistant?" She wipes the liquid iron off her finger on her new dress. The females broke the lock on my case and have taken to wearing whatever they found inside. I've looted a lot this past cycle. There's plenty of shit everywhere. Which reminds me. I need a caravan and more horses. Having females traveling with the horde isn't the same as just us males traveling. We need a horse. Females, and children, one day, will need more than the basics. If I can, I'd like to prepare for when that happens before it happens.

The sister worries her bottom lip. "I've noticed you haven't eaten in a while."

"We fast before the full moon."

"And feast on the full moon?"

"Among other things." We also mate, but that's none of her business.

"When you all grow hungry, make it quick and don't consume me in front of her."

"I have no intention of consuming you, female." If I

96

have a nonmagical mate, this female might be a mate as well, and if that's the case, I'm keeping her. Besides, my mate would be devastated if I devoured her sister. It's wrong in many ways. Though, I bet she's tasty. Standing, I approach and sniff her hair. "Did you use my soap?"

"You mean the soap you stole from Mr. Keirne's shop? Don't deny it. I can smell his soap-making quality."

"Is that where it came from? I have no idea."

She snorts. "You were too busy destroying the village."

"Wasn't me." I wink and get into my furs. The second I do, my mate's body grows taut and rigid. I ignore her instinct to recoil from me and scoot closer so that her back touches my front. Her body's unusually warm. I would worry she's sick if I didn't scent the pheromones she's emitting. I didn't think the king's people entered moon fevers like our females do, but mine is starting to show signs of fever, her body preparing for mating.

I sneak my hand under the furs and touch her bottom, squeeze. "Are you feeling well?"

My mate doesn't answer.

"Are you feeling well?" I repeat. Is there a way to record myself and play it for her every time I've repeated myself? I could probably carve a special sigil just for that purpose. This way, it would save me the trouble. "Female," I purr at her ear, "I always get what I want, and persistence is my nickname, so I will have you speak with me whenever I feel like having a conversation with you. Answer me."

"You talk too much," she says.

"I talk very little." Compared to my brother. But I don't say that. She doesn't know him anyway, though when we meet at the gates of Lyan, she will, because my mate is now a part of my horde. I just have to take great care of how and when I will announce the news I've taken on one of the king's females as a mate. "I reckon I don't have to talk at all." I kiss her shoulder. "I can also run my mouth elsewhere. I'm sure you will like it."

Quietly, her sister leaves my tent, taking the small brown sack with her. I chuckle. Fucking fairies. Can't resist shiny jewelry. Thankfully, my mate isn't one. I nibble on her round ear as I run a finger between her ass cheeks. The sigil on my chest heats, its powerful magic zapping my body, making my cock erect in a fine long rod that pokes her bottom. Spreading her ass cheeks, I nestle my cock right between them. Moving her hair away from her neck, I kiss behind her ear. She shivers, and I keep kissing her there until I notice she's breathing heavily, a tiny moan escaping her lips.

"I give you a gold star for effort. You almost made me think you don't want to fuck me, but there are forces more powerful than your will that will draw you to me. You will surrender to my touch. You will seek my touch, so all this reluctance is a waste of effort and time."

"Says the guy who wants to get in my pants."

"You're not wearing pants." Females have taken to wearing pants. Awful fashions that make the pussy inaccessible. Mine is naked, so I'm doing pretty well for a guy who hasn't flirted in centuries.

"How old are you?" I ask.

"Thirty-seven."

I'm not gonna tell her my age, and I hope she never asks. "Of ripe childbearing age. Mmmm." I swipe a finger over her pussy. It's so wet that it coats my entire finger. Nice, just how I like her pussy. Wet and able to coat my finger with her natural juice, so when I press it against her tiny hole, I lubricate it.

My mate swallows again. "I'm well past childbearing age."

"Says who?"

"Experts."

"Their opinion is noted and promptly discarded."

She giggles.

It's a nice sound. I grab the back of her thigh and push it up to make more room for my cock to glide between her legs. Lightly, I graze her folds with my tip. I'll get her used to my size now so that when the full moon strikes and I mount her, detaching my sigil from the tip of my cock and claiming her as a mate, she'll be ready and begging for it. Picturing myself mounting her and mating her for life makes my cock spout seed on her thigh. I swipe at it and press my thumb over her lips. "Taste me."

My mate flicks the tip of her tongue and tastes a tiny bit. That won't do. I force my finger between her teeth and deposit my seed on her tongue.

"Suck on my finger and taste my seed like you hunger for it." I roll her nipple. It perks up, hardens, and I want to have it in my mouth. And so I tuck her under me. Gold flecks of magic dance in her brown eyes. Stunned, I push up and stare. The flecks disappear, and I blink, then bark, "Open your eyes."

"They're open."

"Open wider."

"My eyes?"

"Yes, your eyes."

She widens her eyes, and I lower my body on top of hers, staring at them. I swear to the great goddess I saw flecks of magic. Such flecks tell the male that the horde female is starting her moon fever, but this is not a female of my kind. She is of the king's people.

But she is also my mate.

Her sigil on my chest yearns for her, wanting us to get closer and mate even before the full moon.

Andy traces my lips with a clawless finger. "There's something wrong with me. I think I'm feverish."

I sniff, and the scent of her arousal stuffs my nose. "You're not sick."

"How do you know?"

"I can smell spoiled food." And your moon fever.

"Oh my fuck." Andy covers her face and laughs. "You really are a predator. This is crazy."

"It is. I think we should stop talking."

"I think not." She peeks between her fingers. With one hand, I secure her wrists above her head, then dip my mouth so it touches hers. I like kissing her and lying on top of her. The heat emanating from her body excites me, makes my cock leak, and my sigil hot at the tip, ready to detach and imprint on her womb.

I kiss her more, even though her mouth is closed. I even let her keep her mouth closed for now and trail kisses down her jaw, neck, shoulder. Like a balm for my senses, her feminine scent soothes and arouses me at the same time. Pleased with how I feel when she's under me, I purr, letting her know she makes me happy.

I must make her happy too, because her hips lift, and she rubs her wetness against my cock. I trail my mouth from her shoulder and down, reach the top of her swollen breast. Before I lick the nipple, I kiss it and trap it between my lips, then I pull. The female moans, her left leg lifting. I grab it and secure it over my hip so I can settle between her legs and lick the nipple.

She fists my hair. "Oh my lord."

I lick again, and she shivers, hips lifting again. She wants my cock.

"In a moment," I say and move on to the other breast, licking that one while rolling her right nipple between my claws. I'm careful not to bleed her, but also, the sharp claw over her nipple provides an element of edge play for me. And maybe even for her, because she lifts her head and watches as I circle my claw around her areola.

The scent of her arousal fills my home. I inhale a lungful and purr as I lick my way down her belly and over her mound. The odor of my mate is strongest here, and my mouth salivates. I swallow as if I'm already tasting her while I spread her legs and lick from the tiny hole at the back all the way to the little bud, where I pause and flick it several times.

My female rests her small feet on my shoulders. I grab the backs of her thighs and push her legs up so I can have easier access to her pussy and ass, both of which I intend to penetrate. It's unfortunate the goddess didn't give me two cocks. She did, however, bless me with a long thick tongue.

But first the fingers. Before I use them inside her sensitive body, I retract the claws. With my index finger, I swipe the slit and gather up the liquid she's made and spread it over her tiny back hole. I massage there before pushing a finger in and slowly pulling out of it.

The female tightens her muscles and ceases breathing.

"Relax and breathe in and out." I withdraw my finger a bit as she inhales, and then I push inside as she exhales. Her pussy spurts more liquid that trails down her slit and onto her ass, where I can use it to lubricate the hole I'm gonna fuck soon. Before I penetrate the small hole, I stick my fat tongue out and lick her pussy, lapping at it like a starving male.

Her breathing is rhythmic now, and I finger fuck her pucker hole faster, retracting the claw of my middle finger before adding it inside. My mate sighs, not in pain, but in pleasure, and I slowly stretch her asshole, again bringing my mouth to her slit, but this time I don't lick the slit, I pay attention to the bud at the top. It's swollen and begging for attention.

The moment I swipe over it, the female shudders. "Your tongue prickles."

She likes it.

I lick again and close my mouth over her clit, sucking and flicking it, watching her, waiting for the flood of pussy juice that's coming. With two fingers in her ass, I press my thumb over the entrance of her pussy, and she pushes against it, wanting it inside, her breathing faster, her moans echoing in the space.

It's fortunate my males hear us, for I want them to understand where I'm coming from and what I see in our future. If there's one king's female whose mating sigil is on my body, there will be other females for them, and other females mean our people will not have to hide in hibernation in order to preserve our population. When we retake the capital from the king, we will spare some of his people, especially the females who would give us young.

My mate's body thrashes, so I'm flicking my tongue at the speed I would use to lap up fresh blood from the wounded body of one of her kind. She fists my hair and lifts her hips, forcing me to stop. I oblige.

There's a moment where nothing happens, like the quiet before the storm, and then her pussy spasms and the female screams, forcing the liquid out of her. It spills all over my chin, and I get to work drinking it up, purring my lungs out as she comes and comes, my fingers in her ass pumping fast.

Her eyes are closed, and she's wrung out, but still her pussy is spasming. Pussy knows best.

Fisting my cock, I kneel before her and bring my dick to her asshole. My thick cock with the glowing red sigil at the top looks beautiful pressed against her small hole. Slowly, I push inside her ass. When the hole resists because it's too small to fit my cock, I force my way inside in the same way I'm gonna force my way inside my mate's heart. One screaming orgasm at a time.

As the head of my cock pushes inside and her ass grips my length, the female's eyes snap open and the magic flecks appear again.

She's fucking beautiful.

And mine.

And I am never letting her go.

CHAPTER
FOURTEEN
ANDY

The savage is fucking me in a place I've never been touched. As I watch the muscles of his torso undulate while he moves his thick cock inside my ass, a part of me is excited and aroused again. But the other part of me sees the strangeness of his golden eyes, the wide nose that flares out with each thrust, and the upper lip that lifts as he picks up speed. The sharp canines remind me he's not a man.

His purr turns into a growl, and I hitch a breath.

He covers my mouth so I'm forced to breathe through my nose. This close, I can smell him, and his scent is masculine and strong, makes me feel safe, but the look on his face terrifies me. He's grunting as he ruts on top of me with a lip that's peeled back, showing all his teeth, and a nose that's flared so he can scent us both. His ears twitch when I squeak out a sound as the feel of his cock makes my belly flutter and my eyes roll to the back of my head.

"Your little fuckhole is my new favorite place. You know what I like to do to places I want? Plow them. Your little pussy is next. It's your jewel, the place males aren't allowed without permission. I specialize in entering without permission. I'm going to pillage your pussy and steal your jewel. Tell me, female, do you like what I'm doing to you?"

He pistons into me, and I can't think. My body's flaming hot, my breasts bouncing up and down, my pussy fluttering, and I need him to get me off right now.

"Do you know what else I'm gonna do? Right after I plow and pillage?"

I shake my head, and he removes his hand from my mouth so he can kiss me. This time, I open my mouth and let him. This seems to set him off, and he snarls as he kisses me, frantically trying to fuck me harder. I'm coming and screaming and he's swallowing my screams while rutting on me until he stills just before he comes.

A jet of seed gushes inside me, and when the male withdraws from me, I'm spent and lie there content to sleep the entire turn away. Head bowed, Tolei kneels, hands on his hips, the sigil on his chest pulsing bright gold. Between his legs, his cock proudly stands and leaks semen.

He presses a palm over the sigil.

"You said that wasn't your sigil," I say into the awkward silence that happens after people have sex like this for the first time. Although, most people have regular sex first and then in-the-ass sex. Tolei doesn't care what others consider normal or regular.

He looks up from the sigil. "Mmhm."

As if anticipating the answer, my cheeks flare with heat before I ask, "Whose sigil is it?"

"Yours."

Swallowing, I don't know what else to say. I wish he'd say something, because I'm feeling awkward as fuck. "I don't have a sigil, Tolei."

"You do."

"How?"

"It's a long story," he says and scrubs his beard. "One I've been looking forward to telling you since I met you. It has bothered me that you have not inquired about the mating or the sigil at all. Why haven't you asked me this before when I had more time to answer?"

"You have time now."

"We need to keep moving."

"Will we ever stop for more than a night?"

"We will stop at the gates of the city of Lyan. We will stop for however many nights it takes until the king is dead and the city is ours."

I scramble up and kneel before him. "You're kidding." Tolei doesn't smile, so I continue. "If you ride up to the gates, the king will destroy you."

"I am offended you think me weak."

"I don't think you're weak."

"Perhaps I have not showed you strength. You will join me in a raid. We shall reach a town before Lyan where the king has set a trap for us. Instead of leaving you behind, you will join me."

"Nah, I'm good."

"I insist. My mate thinks me weak."

"You are the fiercest person I've ever met."

Tolei raises an eyebrow.

"But the king commands armies of thousands of men, and he has powerful magic. My father said the king slays with a flick of his wrist."

"It's hundreds of thousands of men. The king has no magic. And your father is right. All it takes is a flick of a wrist."

"The king has magic, Tolei."

"The king. Has. No. Magic." Tolei barks the words. "The magic is not his. It is stolen, mined, misguided, misused, and I'm gonna kill him for what he's done to my people."

I frown. "Your people?"

"Mine. All of them were once mine." Tolei stands and yanks on his pants.

"Wait." I grab a fur and wrap it around me just as he heads outside, barefoot and bare-chested. We're on the other side of the mountain, heading more inland and north, where it's colder.

"You'll catch a cold," I yell after him and then realize I'm not cold either. I'm sure I'm sick.

"Neither of us will catch a cold. We've entered the mating fever that will last until the night after the moon is full." Tolei points out. "I will mount you and breed you then."

I join him at the tent's exit. "Who are your people? There's no recollection of the horde among my people, or my father would have found you. He's searched all the lands for your horde and never found you. He died telling the king he thinks you're a myth."

"Your father was a miner." Tolei snorts. "My mate is the daughter of a miner. I could've lived my whole life never knowing that."

"He was not. He was a historian."

"Is that what he told you?" Tolei chuckles. "A historian seeking magical creatures, who speaks of a horde that has left the lands and hidden itself for two hundred years is called a Seeker. Your father worked for the king and helped enslave my people, sought out my horde so your king could mine us for magic too." Tolei leaves.

I look up at the bright moon. It bathes my face with its light, and I close my eyes and let the moonlight comfort me. My father was a historian, nothing more, and Tolei is in a

107

bad mood because I offended him when I said the king would slay him at the gates. But the king will slay the horde, if for no other reason than to protect his throne. He won't let Tolei near the gates.

"They say everyone goes crazy during a full moon," a male says.

Startled, I scurry inside the tent, then peek through the flap. Kasei walks out from behind his tent, carrying my father's Big Book. I dislike him for keeping my sister in shackles and always arguing with Tolei. Also, the other horde males hardly ever look at me, but this one sneaks in glances here and there, and I don't like how he looks at me, for malice projects from his gaze.

Unwilling to comment, I retreat into the tent.

Something heavy thuds on the ground.

"It's all in here," he says. "Tolei will never let you go. He will bind you and breed you until the end of time. When he's done with you, you won't know where he begins and where you end. You will lose yourself in him."

"Go away."

"Leave while you still can."

I approach the tent's flap and listen. When I think the male has left, I peek outside and find the book he's left.

I pick it up and sit on the furs, flipping it open slowly, taking care not to damage the pages. It's the only thing I have left of my father's. That and my writing. I inherited the gift of writing and drawing from him. It's just that life has never been easy for us and it took a turn for the worse after he died, and I neglected my talents. Got busy surviving by running the inn with Mag.

I haven't gone through this book since I was a kid, but I remember the pictures of creatures of magic, and I flip through past the fairies and many other magical creatures and reach the last few chapters where my father portrays medeisars as horse-sized four-legged creatures that can walk on either two or four legs. When I was a kid, I skipped these pages because Father drew medeisars as he saw them on the battlefield: hunched over dead bodies, eating the men's guts while the men begged for mercy.

Even now, as a grown woman, I rush through the pages depicting the king's victories because the images of those battle scenes scare me. Toward the end, I spot newer drawings, ones I haven't seen before, and in pencil, not colored yet. It's a drawing of a group of men, huddled around something in the middle. They wear loose pants under fur, leathers, and weapons. They braid their hair with jewelry, and their legs are long and bent backward.

It's the horde. I think Father found them or at least found someone who knew of them, so then why did the king execute him in the square? Mag and I were shamed and shunned after that. Luckily, the inn served outsiders, not just the few people who lived in the village, so we could still feed ourselves.

I lift the paper, trying to figure out what they're hunched over, when the air in the room changes and a shiver runs down my spine. I hear the thing in the tent with me, its breathing rough and heavy, that of a wild animal ready to pounce. I dare not move. I dare not look up. My hands start shaking, and my heartbeat is so loud, I'm sure it'll wake the dead.

The animal growls low in its throat.

It'll pounce and kill me.

I know it the same way I know Tolei always leaves me his boot knife. I glance at it, lying beside the furs, an arm's length away, but if I twitch, the animal in the tent will attack. It'll attack anyway, so I better be fast.

I snatch the knife just as the beast lunges. All I make out is short, dark brown fur, big teeth, and claws spread and extended as they descend to rip me open. I scream for Tolei at the top of my lungs, but know there's no way he can save me now even if he wanted to. Medeisars kill without mercy. This is a predator, and I'm his food.

A roar sounds as the medeisar lands on top of me. I assume a fetal position as chaos reigns around me. Males shout, the tent collapses, and more than one medeisar snarls and snaps his teeth. I dare a peek under my arm, and when I see nothing because the tent fell over me, and the medeisar is gone, I start crawling. "Holy fuck, holy fuck-fuck." I'm crawling for what seems like an entire turn before I finally emerge from the tent. Standing, I turn to check out the camp.

A pair of medeisars are fighting inside a circle made of a glowing red sigil. Outside the circle, the horde stands, as does my sister, her eyes wide and her hand over her mouth. Our eyes lock, and Mag starts crying. She rushes toward me and hugs me tightly. "I thought you were dead."

"Not yet."

"Sister," she says, "we have got to leave. Let's leave."

"Now?"

"There's never been a better time. They're all watching the duel, and whoever wins will lead this horde."

"A duel?"

She nods. "They're medeisars, Andy."

"Yeah, I can see that, but if they're fighting each other, let them. Where's Tolei? I'm sure he'll sort this out."

Mag grabs my cheeks between her palms. "Don't freak out, okay?"

"Okay." When she says that, I'm definitely going to freak out.

"Tolei is a medeisar."

I smile. "You've eaten those mushrooms again?" I want some. It would be nice to forget all this and lie down on the grass high as a kite.

Mag's eyes soften. "Kasei attacked you to provoke Tolei."

I shake my head. "A medeisar attacked me."

"I saw Tolei change. From a male to a medeisar. In a flash of red light." She snaps her fingers. "Just like that, he was in front of me while I prepped supper, and then he wasn't. In a flash of light."

I think back to the river, at the lower half of his body, but he can't be a medeisar. "The king owns the medeisars, Mag. You're mistaken."

"I know what I saw!"

"Okay!" I sidestep my sister and rush to the circle, where two beasts fight. The noises coming from them terrify me before I even see how they're fighting. Males part for me, and I see the medeisar with the short, dark brown fur bleeding from his gut, half his intestines hanging out, and the other one ripping open his chest cavity until he finds the heart and roars into the sky.

I make a keening noise at the back of my throat, and the black-furred medeisar snaps his head my way. He's the victor. The other one is twitching under him, opened from gut to throat. Red eyes lock with mine, and oh, by all that's holy, those red eyes look familiar. I've gazed upon them many a span. My head starts spinning, but I can't look away as he digs into his opponent and rips out his heart.

He eats it in two bites.

My belly rises as the medeisar rises on two legs, exposing a patch of red hair surrounding his groin. His long arms hang by his sides, appearing even longer due to his extensive claws. Blood drips from them.

There's a flash of red light, and Tolei stands there in the nude, the sigil on his chest pulsing, his mouth a liquid mess of blood and flesh. He approaches me, and I stick out my knife. Snarling, he grabs the back of my head and presses his mouth on mine, forcing the knife inside his belly. I let go of the handle. I stabbed him. Lord help me, I stabbed him.

Trying to move him away, I push against his chest.

Nothing happens this time, and Tolei won't let go.

Blood coats our kiss, and I keep my eyes open so my head doesn't spin and I don't faint from fear and shock. Tolei kisses my cheek, smearing blood all over it too. He strokes my hair. "There, there, female, don't fear me." He yanks the knife out of his belly and puts it back into my hand, then brings the hand to his throat. "Cut."

I stare at him.

"Do it."

I shake my head.

"Do it!"

I drop the knife and slap him. "Stop telling me what to do. I'm not your pet. I am your mate, and you will treat me as a partner and not the last person in the world to find out you're a medeisar."

Tolei blinks. I continue because, hey, I've lost my shit and have zero fucks to give. Also, I'm having a nervous breakdown, so fuck him and his shit. I poke his chest. "You should've told me."

"After the mating," he says.

"No, now."

"You would have refused the mating."

"I still can. So I suggest you start...groveling."

"Groveling?"

"Yes. I know, I know. It's probably a word that doesn't register in your Alpha brain, but it exists. You had no right to take me from my home, make me like you, and then turn medeisar on me as if it's perfectly normal."

"It is perfectly normal for me."

"Gah!" I stomp off, but don't get very far, because, of course, Tolei snatches me up and throws me over his shoulder. I kick and scream, but he won't let go, even manages to mount his horse with me hanging over his shoulder. Annoyingly agile male.

From horseback, he barks a few orders as he sits me down, trapping my hands under my body with his arms. I wriggle and try to get away, but give up quickly because there's no escaping Tolei. I sniff because I'm crying now, not sure why. I'm not hurt, just so frustrated with him and his lies, and, you know, I did freak out. Rightfully so.

"I will tell you everything," he says as two horde males ride ahead of us. The horde's moving again, and the rest will follow behind.

"Too late for that."

"You would have killed me if you believed that, so stop bullshitting me. A sigil never lies."

"The hell with your sigil."

He clicks his tongue, and the hell horse starts moving. "It's not my sigil."

"I don't want it either." There, I just want to hurt him.

"You don't mean that."

"I mean it."

That shuts him up, and we don't speak the entire night while riding together. I am wide awake and my adrenaline isn't waning even though we're traveling in the thick forest where the moonlight doesn't light the way and I can barely see two fingers in front of me.

We clear the forest and come up somewhere high in the mountains. Lights twinkle in the town nestled in the valley, and beyond the town is Lyan with its high walls and the king's towers, one of which reaches the clouds hovering low above the city.

Tolei speaks in his language, hushed orders, and the horde dismounts. The hell horses start onward toward the town.

"Wait," I say. "What's happening?"

"We need shelter."

"We have tents."

"Food and shelter. You will bathe and stay in a house."

Tolei dismounts the horse and stretches out his arms for me. Forgetting I'm mad at him, I prop my arms on his shoulders, and he helps me down, then holds me close and purrs. "There will be a bed and fluffy pillows, new clothes, food, even ale."

It takes me a moment to put two and two together. "You mean to raid the town."

"Of course. And you will join me."

I shake my head.

Tolei pinches his lips. "Fine."

Shocked, I ask, "Really?" It's fine?

He nods, clearly disliking my decision, but he won't take me on the raid. I don't need to see it, and at the same time, I don't expect he'll change the ways of his horde or himself for me.

Tolei stands before me and inhales, then moves his hair to the right and twirls the end of the braid before pursing his lips.

I stare up at him, expecting something, when he says, "I'm sorry."

I shall faint now.

I tap my ear. "Come again? I've lost my hearing all of a sudden."

He's annoyed as fuck. Once was hard, but to say it twice is positively gonna give him hives. "I'm sorry for how I heralded our mating."

"We're not mated."

Tolei's jaw clenches. "But we will be." He bites his bottom lip. I think he's nervous. I think he's... Well, I think what I say matters to him and he wants to make it right, though I don't think he knows how. He will figure it out. I won't excuse him. I can't back down, because if I do, he'll roll over me again and again.

"After the raid, I'll take you into a secure home and breed you. The clouds hide the moon now, but the moment they clear and the moonlight touches your body, the fever will start again. This time, it will be worse. The sigil burns with your need." He taps his chest.

"It's unfair you can tell when I'm horny, and I can't tell anything about you."

"I'm always horny. The telling is unnecessary."

"And you always have an answer to everything."

He smiles and bends his head as if to kiss me.

I press a hand over his chest and push him away. Magic throws him again, and Tolei grumbles as he lands on his feet at least a dozen paces away. Walking backward, he is smiling as he descends the hill. "I'm definitely fucking you, Andy."

"Will see about that, savage."

He wags his finger. "I'll show you savage." With that, Tolei turns but doesn't rush into the town after his horses have already entered. He lingers on the outskirts. I find that odd.

Mag hurries up to me and holds my hand. "Crazy shit never stops with these guys. What's next? Lyan?"

The horde is entering the town, yet I hear no screams. This must be why Tolei said the king set up a trap for them. And the horde entered the town anyway. Why would they do that? I step forward, but Mag catches my hand. "Where the hell are you going?"

"Tolei said this town is a trap. I have to see...if... What if he gets killed?"

Mag smiles. "Good riddance."

My chest hollows, and I gasp. "No."

Mag's eyes soften. "He must have a magical cock."

"How do you know he has a magical cock?"

"Does he?"

"Oh, you don't know."

"Like, what's it do? Spin and vibrate?"

"I'm not talking about his cock."

"You want to talk about the medeisars."

I shake my head. "I want to..." I pause, listening. "Mag, why is it so quiet?"

She frowns. "I don't know."

We watch the horde raid the town, throwing around abandoned carriages and barrels surely empty of ale. Over the hill on the other side of the town, a man appears. He wears a blue cape, rides a medeisar, and holds up a single sigil on a flagpole. It's the king's sigil, which, up until now, was the only sigil I'd ever known existed.

"Who is that?" I ask.

Mag shrugs. "No clue."

"He's riding a medeisar."

"Yeah, miners do that."

"Picture someone riding Tolei," I tell her.

"I can't."

Everything Tolei hasn't said and the little bit he has said clicks into place. "Exactly."

It doesn't take long for Tolei to spot the man, and the second he does, three sigils pop off his skin and line up in front of Tolei like circular soldiers. The sigils take on a red hue and start spinning, gathering red smoke as they whirl.

Other medeisars start appearing on the hill, moon reflecting over their dark fur, making the contrast between their fur and their huge white teeth and red eyes more prominent, more frightening. Saliva drips from their mouths as they snarl and snap their teeth, the ones on the edges of the lineup that's formed on the hill pacing restlessly, awaiting their master's command.

"Picture Tolei under someone else's command, obeying the king's orders."

"I can't," Mag says.

Tolei advances up the hill. Alone. The sigils he spins grow in size until they're almost as big as carriage wheels. In the town, the horde males arrange themselves in a triangular formation, each one erecting his own single red sigil in front of him as a soldier would hold a shield.

Tolei barks something, and the medeisars, as if they understand, all freeze at once. The large one under the miner tilts his head before turning up his nose. The miner whips the animal across the face, catching the animal's eye. The medeisar snarls, and the miner dismounts and whips him again. The animal leaps and runs for Tolei.

Mag grabs my hand and starts pulling me.

I dig in my heels. "Wait."

"The medeisars will eat through the horde, and then we're next. Let's go, Andy."

"Tolei is their Alpha," I whisper.

"What?"

"Mag, these are his people."

"They're medeisars, The king's beasts."

I shake my head. "You don't understand. Those are all horde males."

"It doesn't matter. We have to leave."

The medeisar galloping down the hill toward Tolei leaps for him. I scream and cover my eyes. A moment later, I peek through my fingers to find Tolei covered in blood and flesh and the medeisar sliced into three parts. Tolei wipes blood off his face and continues standing there, then he smirks and extends his hand, motioning with his fingers, inviting the miner to come.

The miner turns away and disappears from sight, taking the snarling medeisars with him.

I sit on the grass, a hand over my heart as if I can stop it from pounding. "Crisis averted."

Mag crouches before me, green eyes observing me like I'm a strange bug she's never seen before.

"We could've run," she says.

"He would find me."

"Not if we were careful."

I tap my chest the way Tolei would. "The sigil he carries is mine."

Mag frowns. "How is that even possible? You don't have magic, and he was born hundreds of years ago. The horde males are old, very, very old. They existed in hibernation for hundreds of years. He's lying to you, Andy."

"I don't think he is."

Mag swallows. "So, what now? We're...we're gonna take up with the savages?"

"You don't have to."

Mag stands. "Me and you, sister. We stick together. What happened to that?"

"I don't want you to be unhappy because of me. I want you to choose the horde, not have to stay because I'll stay."

"You'll stay?"

I nod. "It feels right. Like this is what I'm supposed to do."

"Travel the lands, you mean."

"Be with him. When I'm with him, I'm...complete."

Mag runs a hand through her hair, her gaze on the forest behind us. "Would you hate me if I left?"

"I could never hate you, Mag."

She hugs me. "I'm sorry, but the males are starting to sniff around me, and if I don't pick one, I'll have no protection, and I can see a woman in the horde needs protection."

"Tolei will protect you. I'll ask him."

Mag shakes her head, tears falling freely down her face. "They have laws. A male claims a single female, and Tolei can't claim two."

"Sure he can."

Mag chuckles. "That's freaky. Even for me."

I hug her again and squeeze. Over her shoulder, in the town, Tolei watches us as the horde sets up camp for the span or however long they plan to stay here. I wonder if he'll let my sister go or send his males after her. I wonder if he'll let Mag walk away. I wonder if under all that muscle and will and brutality is a heart as golden as the sigil on his chest.

"Go," I whisper. "Go with the wind at your heels and find fortune and a good man to settle down with."

Mag kisses my cheek. "We shall meet again when you raid my town. Stop by for ale, hm?"

I sniffle, but the snot won't go back up, so I wipe my nose with my sleeve.

Mag rounds me, and I turn to watch her run up toward

the forest. Before she's lost to me, she turns and waves, her pretty green eyes shining with tears. I wave back, and Mag is gone. Immediately, I feel like someone cut away half my heart and ran off with it.

I walk toward the town and straight for Tolei, who stretches out his arms and then wraps them around me. And I couldn't care less that he's bloody and dirty and has just ransacked a town. He makes me feel safe and cherished and not alone in the world. For most people, that counts for something. For me, having grown up with no mother and having lost my father and now Mag, it counts for everything.

CHAPTER
FIFTEEN
TOLEI

Losing my second-in-command will cost us more males unless I secure the town with well-fortified wards that I'll have to strengthen each span, maybe even twice a span so that the medeisars sense the strong, familiar magic. It should repulse them from attacking us, and that would create a wedge in the king's plan to kill us all while we're still in small numbers.

I expected to find my brother here or near here, but after Neensei returned from scouting the hills and forests, he reported no horde sightings. In the past, my brothers and I used magic to communicate with each other, but we severed our bonds before taking our hordes separate ways and hiding in hibernation. If one horde was found sleeping, the others would be safe from the king's Seekers. Or one particular Seeker, namely my mate's father.

I flip though his book, reading the findings he's collected over the turns, and discover the man thoroughly researched my kind and has a thing or two to teach even me. When you get to be as old as I am, there's not much you haven't seen or heard, so any new information I gather from his book is welcome.

The Seeker went as far as the winter court to seek out information on the horde. One of the fae fuckers must've described my oldest brother's horde, because I'm looking at the picture of my oldest sibling. It's him, his long dark braid secured with a white leather band he removed from our sister's wrist before he laid her body to rest. We never found her head.

Her head is with the king, says the book. He mined it for healing magic and it's still preserved inside his magical laboratory, which is not supposed to exist since the king claims he is the only man with magic, that he's a god, a divine man gifted with magic.

No such thing as a man gifted with magic, even if he is divine.

Heavy footsteps approach the tent, and by the way he walks, I can tell it's Neensei. He pokes his head inside my tent. "You coming?"

Groaning, I rise and leave the book on the furs.

"What are you reading?" he asks.

"A book about us."

"There's a book about us?"

"There is now." I walk with him toward the firepit, where males chat and drink the horrible old ale we found in someone's cellar. The town barely had any supplies, the ale was scarce, and, judging by the rags we didn't even want to steal, poor, its inhabitants long gone either for fear we'd raid or in search of places where they could prosper, not rot.

A little ways away from the horde, Andy huddles on a piece of thick brown fur, alone and looking like a sad puppy, her gaze on the fire. The moon is full and shines on her face, forever etching her beauty into my mind. I crouch beside her, scoop her up along with the fur, and move us closer to the fire.

I put her down and arrange my body around hers. Mist rises and the clouds gather. Thunder strikes in the city. Bad weather is coming for us. Might as well enjoy the dry ground and the fire while we can.

I offer her my fur to wrap around her shoulders, but she shakes her head.

Sweat beads her forehead. Meanwhile, we're all in fur coats.

I kiss the side of her neck, her skin burning my lips. The moon fever is strongest during the full moon. I inhale her arousal just as she wipes sweat from her forehead. "Exiled from Komena, our afterworld, Yerlenia, goddess of love, descended to our mortal realm and stumbled upon a raided horde camp, where bodies littered the ground. The male who sought revenge for the slaughter pleaded with the goddess for strength. She gave him the savage abilities he sought. His name was Leian, and he was the first of my kind."

The horde quiets, and Andy turns her head my way, pulling up her knees and resting her cheek there.

I kiss her temple, then whisper, "You wanted to know. I will tell you everything, king's female, and I will risk the lives of my people with our secrets and my heart. You can have it all. But in return, your pussy will be at my disposal, wet and ready whenever I feel like fucking you."

"Is that all you want from me?"

"Not even close." I also want her to look at me the way she looks at her sister. With love so open and exposed that it disarms me, chips off some of the icicles I've accumulated over my heart during my years of hibernation while I nourished bitterness and plans of revenge. Hate for the king

123

grows strong in me. I had forgotten about love and females and babies.

I also want babies from her. My cock leaks semen, and I pull my mate closer so she can feel my hardness. A blush appears on her cheeks, and my males groan. They all can smell her arousal and mine. They'll do a lot more than smell. They'll also hear her screaming while I rut over her tonight, so they can all fuck off with their grunting and whining and sit there and envy me for the next...well, for the duration of all time, for after she mates, Andy will be linked to my immortality and we shall fuck forever and ever.

"Is there a love story between Leian and Yerlenia?" she prompts.

"Oh yes. There's a book of obscenity for those two."

"I'd read that, but wait. How does it end?"

"Ends in tragedy, I'm afraid."

"Then I won't read it."

"Why not?"

Andy shrugs. "What's the point if they don't live out their lives together?"

I tap my claw on her shoulder. "All right. I won't tell you all their story. Only parts. Yerlenia called upon a strong beast that existed in the goddess's realm called a medeisar and bound the medeisar to the male, merging the two so that they coexist on this plane. One male, two forms. Because the goddess was only fertile during the full moon, that was the only time she could conceive and why a mate to a savage male experiences mating fever. Yerlenia and her savage had many babies. But one night, the goddess of creation, the one married to your Lord King, by the way, came down to check on Yerlenia and found her many children a threat. She slew them all."

"Ensnia did that?"

Tolei nods.

"Not true."

"It is true."

"I've read the Holy Esen, and there's no mention of that."

"Because the Holy Esen was written by followers of Ensnia, and if they mentioned the horrible things Ensnia did, nobody would follow them and donate to their shrines."

"Oh, come on." Andy gives me a skeptical look.

I raise an eyebrow. "This legend of Yerlenia and Leian has been narrated among my people since it happened. Now, Yerlenia sought revenge against Ensnia. She made an army of male savages and set out to avenge her babies. She ravaged the lands until she grew so hateful and powerful that she forgot who always rode by her side."

"Leian."

"That's right."

"Did she kill him?"

"Don't ask questions you asked me not to give you answers to."

Andy nods. "Medeisars are all horde males, then?"

"One can be a horde male and a savage beast at the same time. We are both a male and a savage, but not a medeisar. A medeisar is a term used to describe a creature who is mad and can no longer reason the way we can. When one becomes a medeisar, there's no coming back from the madness. We are horde, savage beasts or males."

"I have a story for you, female," Neensei interrupts and scoots out of my reach like a little pussy. I won't like his tale. I can tell I'm not gonna like it because my males start arguing over which tale to tell. The choices involve me and things they've laughed at that I've done over the long turns we've ridden together. When Neensei shouts he'll tell the one where I got trapped in the sewer and Andy perks up from her seat and starts giggling at their theatrics, I call it a night.

Having Andy's attention got to their heads, and now they all want a piece of it. Well, I do not share. Not even her attention. Nope.

Rising, I scoop her up. "Goodbye."

Boos follow me inside the big white house I've picked as my home tonight. The one with a nice fancy bed propped on a wooden frame and a headboard she can hold on to while I mount her.

Once inside, I set her on her feet, and she looks around the spacious entryway, even touches the tiny stones of the mosaic I'm stepping on. I remove my fur, my tattered shirt, the belts and weapons, and the kilt over my pants, I rip. Releasing my cock from the constraints, I sigh and watch the beast spring free and leak semen. I give him a few strokes, then scoop up some seed, and when Andy stands, her eyes wide and shocked, I swipe my thumb over her lips.

I don't give a fuck what she says or does, those flecks of gold in her eyes and the sigil pulsing in my chest tell me everything I need to know. The moon touched her face, and she has a fever only I can cure. "If you swoon now, you'll fall right on my dick."

Andy shakes her head and moves toward the kitchen as if to explore the house.

"The bedroom is upstairs," I announce.

"I'm looking for a bathtub in the back."

"Female, please. I already found the tub and got it ready."

Andy returns with a smile on her face. "That's nice."

"I grovel with the best of them, no?"

"That's not groveling."

Well, fuck. "But it will get me laid."

Andy smiles wider. "You're a hopeless case."

I like this look on her. Feverish and red in the face and also smiling. It's a good look on her. Tonight, I will make her forget about her sister, if only temporarily. She'll be sad tomorrow, but as time passes and the moon cycles spin, she will become with child, and have more children, and we shall travel more lands, and she will be better for it.

After I kill her king.

CHAPTER
SIXTEEN

ANDY

As I climb the stairs, I make sure I touch the many things that make this house everything I hoped I'd experience some span. The various textures between different materials that make up the wall tapestry. The iron swirls of the staircase railing. I pause and kick off my sodden boots and remove my holey socks, swearing I will wear finer things from now on because when Mag left, old Andy left too.

I no longer need to be poor.

I wish to see, touch, explore, liberate myself of only dreaming about things and never doing anything about my dreams. Father always said he'd take me with him, but he never meant it. I was his housekeeper. Mag and I. We kept his inn, brought in the money he'd collect when he returned from travels seeking this very horde, this very male to enslave into the king's service.

Meanwhile, neither Mag nor I have any clue who our mothers were, and in retrospect, I see how he conditioned us not to ask those types of questions. We asked, sure, but the answer was a counterquestion. He'd ask if we needed a mother. We'd say no, because how would we know if we needed something we never had? In our own way, we were trapped in hibernation, going about our spans doing the same things over and over again, dreaming about lands beyond our village and how we'd one span have enough money to see them all.

Turns out, I don't need coin to see the lands.

Turns out, the horde sees everything and wants for nothing. They're free to roam even through other people's homes. I enter a bedroom, and the first thing I see is a large barrel of water that people use as a bath. Vanilla candles Tolei lit up all over the room create a pleasant mood, and the fireplace adds a lovely touch of intimacy.

"Swoon," I say as I strip off my clothes. I practically jump into the bath, then cross my arms and grab my shoulders. "I froze."

Tolei dips a claw into the bath, and one sigil detaches from his arm. This close to the magic, I'm transfixed, curious what the sigil will do. It twirls in the water and returns to Tolei's arm.

The water turns hot, steam rising from it.

Tolei joins me and flips me around so I'm nestled between his legs and my back rests on his chest. The sigil there warms my back, adding more heat to my already feverish body. I begin to sweat. Tolei grabs a small towel, lathers it with soap, and starts washing me, from the neck down my belly and between my legs. He picks up my left leg under the knee and throws it over the edge of the tub, rubbing my pussy with the wet towel. I squirm as he purrs, then he yanks my hair and turns my face toward him so he can watch me. He doesn't kiss me, though I want to kiss him.

I edge toward his face, but he holds me immobile with a

fist wrapped around my hair. One hand lifts my bottom, and he positions me over his erect cock. Slowly, he pushes me down on top of his cock so all his length enters me at once. Moaning, I close my eyes as he moves me over his cock, my channel so wet that his length glides in despite the size of him. The pace is slow and enticing, telling me Tolei knows how to be a gentle lover.

He kisses me, and I open my eyes to see his are also open, the color of melting gold. I could get lost in them, in him, and so I look away. He breaks the kiss and holds my jaw tightly so I can't move my face or look away while he lifts my bottom over his cock, the pace faster now, water splashing around us.

"Your sigil tells me how you feel about me, about us, before you or I even know what's happening between us. I can feel your joy, love, sorrow, and other feelings I've never experienced before. They're addictive, and therefore, I want more of them. I want your everything." He impales me on him and holds me there by my hip, then starts rising from the bath with me on his cock. We don't disconnect when he bends me over the water and tells me to hold the edge of the tub so he can fuck me from behind.

Claws dig into my hips, and I tuck my hand between my legs and rub my clit while his balls slap my ass until I come and my knees fold. Tolei holds me up and uses my body any way he needs it. The stream of seed heats up my channel once more and makes me cum again.

My hands shake as I grip the edges of the tub.

Tolei picks me up and moves to the bed. Eyes still molten gold, he's as sexy as ever with mussed hair and braids that are coming undone as he positions himself between my legs and moves over me. When I touch his face, he growls and increases his pace. I bite his lip, and he stops briefly, closes his eyes, and grips my throat, squeezes.

"Why do you poke the savage in me?" he asks. "I'm trying to be what you need me to be."

"I want you to be you," I whisper and bite harder.

Tolei growls against my lips, making them vibrate.

He flips me around and presses a palm over my back so I can't move. His cock enters me, bigger somehow this time, and that's when I see his hand land on the bed near my head to prop up his weight.

I shut my eyes and surrender to the savage's touch.

TOLEI'S LIMBS WRAP AROUND ME SO I CAN'T MOVE, AND EVEN IF I could, I'm not sure I know where I end and he begins. We're intertwined, the heat of our bodies keeping us warm while I stroke his cock, running my thumb over the mushroom top with no sigil. His sigil is inside me, branding me as his mate.

My sigil spins above us, a massive golden pulsing light that drips flecks of pure magic onto our naked bodies. I blow a fleck that lands on his shoulder, and like ash, it flies off, dispersing in the air.

On his chest, I trace the indentation the sigil makes when it leaves his skin.

Tolei makes a strange noise.

I glance up at him. "Does this hurt?"

"No."

"What is it, then?"

"It tickles."

I smile. "Why, mighty savage, are you telling me you're

ticklish?" I trace two fingers over the soft skin where the sigil resides.

Tolei bats my hand away.

I return to stroking his skin, and he rolls his eyes.

"Fine, have at it," he says.

"Will it return?"

He frowns. "The sigil?"

"Yeah. Will it return or do I get it or will it hover above us for all eternity?"

"It returns to me." I'm clueless about his magic, and he has to let me in on these secrets of his people that no books have been written about, that the king surely must not know or he'd have found a way to use.

"I would like to know more about you."

He quirks an eyebrow. "Is that so?"

"It is."

Tolei licks his lips. "I have a story again."

I nod, eager to hear it.

"There once lived a horde male who other horde males feared. On a particularly harsh winter night, in search of food, he took his horde farther away from camp than he normally would. When he returned, he discovered that some men had slain his wife and all the females in the camp. They slayed the children, the pets, the animals. Everyone. He swore revenge, and as a reminder of his dead female, he carved her name inside a circle on his chest.

"His sorrow," Tolei continues, "reached Yerlenia, goddess of love, who appeared before him. She offered him a way to avenge his female, but under one condition. That he helped her ascend back to the realm of the gods. He agreed. She bound him to her with the sigil on his chest, became his mate, and turned him into her personal pet. His horde fared the same. Now they had powerful magic and a way to kill and consume the enemy, but they were also at Yerlenia's mercy, doing her bidding."

"And you still pray to Yerlenia?"

"Yes, she is our goddess of creation as much as Ensnia and the Lord King are yours."

"Then what happened?"

"I thought you didn't want to hear the story."

"Give me the happy version."

Tolei purses his lips. I want to bite them. They're plush and soft, and he's a good kisser.

"The happy version is... One of the horde males found his mate, separated from the original horde, and escaped the fate of the original horde when Yerlenia grew bored."

"Hmm, so how is the king controlling medeisars?"

"I don't know. I don't believe I will ever know, for that knowledge shall die with him. If I were him, I'd tell nobody, and I presume he hasn't."

"Can you guess?"

Tolei nods. "Because we were created as Yerlenia's personal pets, there must be some way he tapped into that part of us that seeks another and used it to make them his own pets. He had to have found spells of old, likely from the fae fuckers that record such things."

"Can he enslave you?"

Tolei's eyes switch to red from gold in an instant. "Not anymore."

"But he could before?"

"One cannot belong to a king if one is claimed by another."

I chuckle. "You're making it sound like I claimed you."

"You didn't?" He rears back, sounding offended now.

He's so grumpy. "I did." I nod and push against his chest so I can straddle him. With one hand, I support my weight while I put his cock inside me with the other. It stretches and fills me, and I close my eyes, throw back my head, and moan as I ride him. Having sex with Tolei is like walking into fire and knowing you won't get burned. The savage beast inside him makes him unpredictable and fierce, but all that fierceness also means he's a forceful lover who fucks hard and loves harder.

"Do you love me?" I ask him as I glide over his cock, my heart beating a mile a minute when Tolei presses his lips together.

"Falling in love is easy," I say, and continue despite his growling. "The hard part is when you love someone who doesn't love you back."

"Your sigil doesn't lie. I know you love me."

I swallow. "That's the issue. I don't have any reassurance that you feel the same way. It would be nice if I did."

Tolei grabs the back of my neck and pulls my body on top of his. "You are my mate, Andy. When the going got hard for my horde because of your king, I got harder, but I never stopped loving you, even when the idea of you brought me pain." He grabs my hips and starts moving me over him, one hand gripping my throat. "Love is a nice, average word to describe how I feel about you. I do love you, Andy."

"You have a better word that describes how you feel about me?"

He squeezes my throat, won't let me breathe while he makes me fuck him harder. "Adore."

Damn.

SEVENTEEN

I blessed every surface of my new home with Andy's cum and wrung every drop of her energy until she couldn't stand. Then I let her sleep a little before I took her again. And again. What can I say? I'm horny, and my mate's pussy is sweet and tight, and I could mate her for a cycle, but rising from the bed now seems a burden for Andy.

She duck walks with her legs far apart, wincing on her way to the bathroom.

"Mmhm." I nod in approval and prop my head on my hand. During the mating of a male and a female, the abundant magic of the mating sigil protects the horde from invaders, which is the only reason I'm able to fuck Andy for the next two spans and not worry about a pack of medeisars circling my camp.

Those could be former members of my horde and I wouldn't know it, and while it's not particularly important who they were when they were sane, I would like to know who I'm killing so I can pray for their safe passage to the afterlife. I have to kill my own kind before I can get to killing the king, and I can't even bid them a farewell.

The magic linking the savage to their Alpha in the horde pulses on each male of my horde, but the king broke those links, severed all magical sources from the savage beast, keeping them as medeisars forever.

The transformation can't be overturned. At least not by me. I will have to kill everyone who stands in my way on my way to Lyan's palace. I dream of that beautiful sunny span when we breach the gates, climb over the walls, and slay everyone who stands in the way to the throne, where the king will fight me and lose.

I bet my brothers dream of the same span.

And that's why I expect them to arrive and meet me here. I alone cannot take down the king, only because he has placed medeisars in my way. I feel them circling the camp, snarling beasts testing the wards I erected around us. Each time one of them gets close to my wards, the king's dark magic, like slime, slithers across my senses.

My mate's sigil spins near the celling, and I stare at it, bracing for the force of its magic when I call it to return to me. Maybe later. I don't want to scream like a little pussy in front of my mate, and I'll scream for certain. The influx of new power has to burn through me before I can use it. There's a price for playing with powerful toys, and a mating sigil is a powerful toy.

What price is the king paying? There's something, and if I can figure out what, I'll be better prepared for our final conflict. I could use it against him.

Andy emerges from the bathroom, her breasts swollen, nipples red, her hips showing bruising. There're at least three claw marks on her thigh. I really am a fucking savage.

"Are you in pain?" I ask.

"Sore down there." She blushes prettily and averts her gaze.

"Baby, I've fucked your ass, pussy, and mouth. What is there to be embarrassed about anymore?"

She sighs. "You know what, Tolei?"

I brace. "What?"

"Practice diplomacy."

"Okay." I sit up, listening. I would do anything for her. Groveling confused me, but this I'm gonna handle. I've got this. "What is it?"

"It's when you find better words to describe something that isn't so blunt so the emotional impact on another person is lessened."

"I love you," I say.

Andy blinks.

"There. The emotional impact is lessened."

She shakes her head.

"You said to practice diplomacy. I was diplomatic."

"Suddenly throwing those three words at me is emotionally impactful."

Agreeing, I grab her and tuck her under me. She spreads her legs and looks at me like I'm her personal god. Sore or not, she's ready to please me. I know I'll have to take care with that pleasing nature of hers.

"I will always look out for you and protect you. You're immortal now and will live for as long as I live."

Andy's eyes are saucers. "Seriously?"

"Mmhm." I kiss her nose as the king's magic melds into my wards, testing my defenses. It feels like I swallowed spoiled food, and I taste iron at the back of my throat. I have to go and reinforce the wards, cleanse them of the king's dirt. "Stay inside the wards," I whisper at her ear. "No matter what you hear or see. Stay inside the wards."

I dress and leap out the window, landing on the street and walking toward the hill where Neensei strolls, already sensing the king's magic mixing with mine. On the other side of the wards, a pair of medeisars walk in mirror image of him, their red eyes watching his every move. They foam at the mouth at the prospect of a full meal. They don't know they'll be eating their own flesh and blood.

"You think this one is my brother?" Neensei asks, pointing.

I wince. "Your brother is dead."

"Hopefully." He grabs my ax, and I rest a hand over it where he grips my ax's handle.

His red eyes glow fiercely as they meet mine. "Promise me you'll kill me. You won't let him tame me, ride me, make me his bitch."

"I promise."

He nods. "Also, you smell like pussy."

"Thank you."

"Welcome. Did you play with the new sigil?"

"Not yet?"

"Pussy."

"Quit saying that word."

"Rolls nicely off my tongue."

"Quit using it."

"You're still cranky, I see. I hoped the mating would give you a personality transplant."

"I don't know why you'd hope that when I already have a great personality."

"You're worse than before."

"But I am mated."

Neensei laughs.

The medeisars circle the camp, the king's slimy magic rubbing me all wrong, irritating me, and the iron from his dirty magic collects at the back of my throat, making it hard to swallow. I need my brothers so they can share the burden of holding off the king and strengthening our wards. The king would be stupid not to attack now, when the threat is only a few horde males. He will attack. I don't know when, but I can only prepare and hold position until my brothers arrive.

"You gonna be a pussy or accept her sigil back?" my male asks.

I flip him off and walk the perimeter of the circle to ensure there aren't any wide cracks in the wards where the medeisars can enter. As I circle, the medeisars follow me, snarling. I snarl back, wanting to wring their necks and collect their claws so I can make a necklace for my pretty mate. I wonder if she'd prefer their teeth? Hmm. I'll ask later.

I steal a few glances at the house and see Andy at the window. I make sure she's well before I call on the horde. We huddle together as I draw a sigil and step inside it. Outside it, the horde males push out their shielding sigils so the magic I'm about to receive doesn't hurt them. We don't have a clue what kind of magic a mating sigil will provide, but we know it's powerful, the kind of magic that can topple kings.

When I first set out to kill the king, I was going to do it with my own two hands and what magic I already had. But the goddess smiled on me and put me on a path that crossed with my mate. Blessed, I kneel and spread out my arms, then call the mating sigil back.

It crashes into my chest with such force that it takes my breath away. I gasp, eyes snapping wide open as the magic burns all the way through my body, making my bones grind, my muscles spasm, my entire body shake violently. My teeth clench and some crack as I lock my jaw tightly, because if I don't, I'll scream like a pig on slaughter day. Tears wet my eyes.

"He shall cry," Neensei says and leans over me. "Twenty golds on a sobbing Alpha here. Any takers?"

Oh, that little bitch.

I hold back the tears that are coming because my fucking brain is burning, and tear glands do what they will on their own.

"Oh, oh." Neensei points. "A tear. I see it."

He's gonna pay for making fun of me while I'm burning alive. "I will kill you, boy," I grit out, and my tooth wobbles and falls out.

Neensei picks it up. He holds it up like a fucking trophy. "I got his tooth!"

My balls start expanding. *Oh, fuck no, magic. Don't go there.* My cock burns and grows erect, and pain zaps my lower belly, bending me over. My forehead touches the ground as I hold my middle and groan. The pain is terrible. I will die like some turd on the dirt.

"Tolei?" Andy says.

Fuck me. "Hm?" I mutter, still bent over and unable to look up or even move. Magic seizes my body, doing whatever it wants with it, mainly making my blood boil.

"What's wrong with him?" she asks.

"He's receiving the mating sigil."

"Is it normally like this?"

"We don't know what it's normally like."

"Can it hurt him?"

"Awww. You're worried about him," a male voice I haven't heard in centuries says. Maybe I didn't hear correctly. Maybe I'm delusional and feverish, and maybe I've gone crazy, unable to hold the power inside me.

The male crouches in front of me, and I sniff.

Snapping my head up, I almost break my neck. But it's worth it. My brother is here. Slei wears red fur over his shoulders, and his hair is loose with a few braids holding back his silver-gold mane. I forgot how handsome he was, and now I'm upset he's handsome and sharing a camp with my mate.

Slei's red eyes are full of mischief as they roam over my body. Two hundred years, I haven't seen him. As always, his timing is shit.

He strokes my hair and starts braiding a piece of it. "Tolei, I will write you a song."

The horde snickers.

"I will write a song everyone will sing around the fire. We will sing it so loudly, even the king shall hear it all the way in the palace. The world will hear how you shivered like a wet kitten when you got magic." He whispers at my ear, "From a king's female, of all females."

"Fuck you."

Slei rises and throws his arm over Andy's shoulders, then kisses the top of her head. "You're so small and cute," he says. She tries to get away, but he won't let her.

"I will kill you," I bite out. I stand, magic still burning through me, but in a different way. It feels like power. Pure power, a tingling burn at the tips of my fingers making my skin want to peel off my body.

"What kind of magic burns the skin and makes my body brim with power?"

"Fire magic," Slei answers.

I shake my head. "What else?"

A glow peels off my skin, the magic so pure, it's golden. I touch it, and it's hard, almost as if it's metal itself.

"This is battle magic," I say. "More battle magic."

His eyes widen as he releases my mate, then throws his

hands about my body and brushes his cheek against mine. He smells like...like ass, probably hasn't bathed since he woke up from hibernation.

"You smell like an asshole."

He punches my shoulder. "And you like a rose petal."

The males laugh.

"It's lavender, not rose," I say.

They laugh harder.

Andy stands back, smiling but looking uncomfortable. I walk to her and grab her hand, intertwining our fingers the way her sister might. I'm not her sister, but I will have to do for her. The magic of her sigil delivered to me more of who I am and what I most wanted. Strength and the ability to preserve the few males I have left while my brothers arrive, and we can regroup and take on the king's vast army.

How appropriate for someone like Andy to give another something she knows will please them most. I thought her sigil would hold the fire, the shadows, the magic of earth, even, but not that it would cater to my particular needs. Her magic is most unexpected, very powerful, and also selfless.

I kiss the top of her hand. "I can only hope to return as much as you've given me with this mating. To be whatever you need me to be. Diplomatic, groveling, and whatever else you want from me. I shall do it."

The king's magic slithers against my senses, and I look above her head to where a medeisar crosses inside my wards. The mad creature howls, and the other medeisars all turn and rush to enter via the cracked spot in the wards.

The horde males start shouting, Andy's pulling my hand toward the house, and Slei's advancing toward the enemy on his own. Where is his horde? Oh fuck. They're outside my wards with the medeisars, fighting them. That damn Acoustico. We can't hear anything, can't catch them attacking unless we're watching, and nobody was watching. They watched me take the mating sigil.

The silence pisses me off. The pressure developing in my ears makes me think my brains might explode. I call after my brother, but of course, he can't hear me, already engaging two medeisars. Fighting a medeisar on two legs is less effective than it would be if we turned into one of them, but we don't, for we have no idea how the king is enslaving them and would like to keep our sanity, thank you very much.

I put Andy behind me. Can't bark orders, but some of my horde males huddle around her as if knowing I want to protect her. We form a circle and let the medeisars come to us. The crack in my wards lets in a dozen creatures and a dozen more are lined up to enter, but they are forced to come in one by one because the crack is small, reminding me of the small entrance I encountered at the cave. And now I know why the entrance was small. It's to hold a medeisar inside. That male I killed up in the mountains had never seen the light of the sun, not since the king trapped him inside and mined him for magic.

Slei's trying to reach his horde while they're running from the medeisars to get inside my wards, and I can't drop my wards because I'll let the medeisars in too. My brother got inside, but that's because he knows how my wards work and how to sneak past them.

A blue robe appears. It's the damn Acoustico.

I will have his head. I call the mating sigil, and because the magic is so powerful and I haven't had a hot moment to learn to control it or even play with it, I lose my grip over it immediately.

Hundreds of spinning blades explode out of my chest.

My horde, having felt me release the magic, dive for the ground, all covering their heads. Out there, Slei dives too, and his horde turns and starts running for the forest because the mating sigil's blades whirl swiftly and travel outward, slicing everything in their path.

In a matter of moments, the sound returns, and pieces of medeisars litter the ground. The sigil's magic spreads, slicing and dicing outside the wards, forcing Slei's horde to run faster or die. I better call the sigil back.

The moment the thought occurs, the sigil returns to me with such force that it throws my body back several paces. I land right on my ass and stay there for a while, stunned at the carnage. The bodies of the enemy litter the ground while the horde males are all accounted for, their boots making sloshing noises as they run toward each other. There's cheering and laughter as brothers, fathers, and cousins are reunited.

Andy kneels before me to take my face between her palms. "Are you okay?"

I kiss her. "Baby, your magic makes me so happy. It killed them all."

Andy smiles uneasily, looking a little pale in the face. The battle, the blood, the slayed medeisars aren't a pretty sight for a lady but she will accept it as a way of life for us until the hordes topple her king.

"The king won't be back anytime soon." I groan as I stand and throw an arm over my mate's shoulder, nudge her toward the blue robe on the ground.

Slei joins us at the Acoustico's body, his hands on his hips. "Hmmm, what to do with the miner?" He gives me a knowing look then glances at my mate.

"What?" Andy asks, her head bobbing between us.

"I'll walk you back to the house," I say because Slei will

burn a horde sigil on the Acoustico's forehead, then remove the head and send the package back to the king. I don't want Andy to witness all that.

Andy pauses and just when I think she'll protest, she nods.

Slei groans. "Why don't I walk Andy back to the house while you fix your wards and the miner."

"I don't think so," I say.

"I'm not going to steal your mate, Tolei."

"I know that." I'm unreasonable when it comes to Andy. I make no excuses for my lack of reason. Turning, we leave.

"Only want to ask if she has a sister."

"She does not," Andy answers, with a side glance directed at me.

I nod at her.

"Your wards are dead," my brother says.

"Fix my wards."

"Tolei," he shouts after me but I ignore him and scoop up Andy before entering the house. She throws her hands around my neck, her brown eyes reflecting the kindness of her heart.

Like she's a bride, I carry her inside the house and put her down.

Andy touches my chest, and the sigil responds by heating my skin. "What will you do with the miner?"

"Nothing."

She traces the outline of the sigil, and I groan as it tickles.

"You want to shield me from some of the horrors of the horde," she says.

"Yes and no," I tell her as she moves to the windows, the ones overlooking the forest. The longing for her sister penetrates my senses. "Mag was seen before the gates of Lyan."

Andy whips her head around. "You had her followed?"

I nod.

"But the risk of getting caught outside the wards..." Her voice trails off. "Is she well?"

I nod. "As well as one can be on her own. I believe she will enter the city." Mag would have stayed if she enjoyed any of my males. But she didn't, and having to constantly deflect unwanted attention tired her out. Andy will need other females in the horde, and soon, as she will start growing with my child.

"We intend to seize that city," Andy says.

For the first time, she said *we* and meant the two of us and the horde. As my chest swells with the love I store for her in my heart, I cross the room and lift her up into my arms. I squeeze her bottom.

Looking down at me, Andy tucks a lock of hair behind her ear. "When we enter Lyan, Mag will have ale ready for us."

"And so we shall drink and celebrate."

Andy cups my face and tilts her head so she can bring our lips together and kiss me softly, gently, the way she often does and I do not. Pulling back, she grabs her braid, which I keep attached to my head and intertwined with my own hair. When she realized I cut off her braid, Andy swore she'd shave my head, but I think she likes how I sport it.

"Why do you wear it still?"

"I like owning a piece of you."

"The sigil isn't enough?"

"It's not my sigil."

Secretly, Andy understands how the mating works and that she owns a magical beast in a way I don't own her. There's freedom in that. With Andy in my arms, I move toward the other windows, the ones overlooking the hill we'll cross one day on our way to Lyan, where I shall liberate my people from the king's tyranny so that my mate and our kids can roam this land as free as the horde is meant to be.

***

Hi,

Milana here. Thank you for reading Tolei and Andy's story. Tolei's voice carried the story wherever he needed it to go so I very much felt like a vessel while writing this fantasy romance, a sub-genre of romance I've just started exploring as a writer, one I've been pleasure reading for a long while.

I hope you will stay on this journey with me, and read book two, which you can start on the next page.

SAVAGE IN THE HEART
TEASER
UPPR

A s a part fairy with round ears, I lived well among the king's people.

That all changed after the savage horde swept through the village and took me prisoner. I escaped the horde, but having to now linger outside the walls of the capital city means I'm homeless, hungry, thirsty, and covered in dirt. I haven't bathed since that one span the soldiers sprayed the homeless outside the gates with the water hose so we didn't stink when the convoy of fae on their fine horses prepared to enter.

Fairies and refugees are the only ones coming and going from this end of the city. Maybe on the south side, trade resumes as normal, but the savage horde's camp can be seen from this gate, and people fear the savages.

For the right reasons too. They *are* savages. Beasts that can turn into predators with a single thought and a flash of their powerful magic.

Ten spans ago, I left the savage horde camp for Lyan, where I planned to find work and put a roof over my head, but I ended up sleeping outside the city walls with a knife in my hand and one eye open. The area along the city walls isn't a good place for anyone, especially not for a woman who is at least one-quarter fae and attracts men even when she doesn't want to.

My mother must've been a fairy, and I inherited some of her features and also the charms. Having never known her, I can't say for sure, and since Father disliked it whenever I asked about her, I never found out who she was.

Not that her identity matters much, but it would explain what happens to most men and savages when they look upon my face. Sometimes they seem enthralled, and I believe I'm drawing them in, but sadly, I don't know how to turn it off.

Or even on. And I'd really like to turn on the charm with a few of the soldiers manning the gates. They're asking for papers to get into the city. Papers I don't have, since I came here with the horde pretty much emptyhanded.

I wished Lyan hadn't closed the gates on refugees from other parts of the kingdom. They're sending us across the sea, and while I'd love to travel, I won't voyage too far from my sister, who's in the savage horde's camp just over that hill.

The king tightened the patrols and security, and getting into the city now is like traveling outside the kingdom. One needs a million papers proving they are who they say they are. I need them quickly, because right after midnight last night, the king issued another law. Outsiders can't get in without an invitation from someone on the inside. I know nobody in the city. I know nobody anywhere. Other than in the horde, but there, I would be a treated like a warm body and handed around from male to male.

After the savages' alpha, who is now my sister's mate, killed one male who I kept refusing, another male started sniffing around me. I'd had enough of them, and when they were busy raiding the town they now call home, I fled.

I miss my sister, I do, but I'm not a horde's mate, so nothing offers me protection or a way of living among them.

Pulling the heavy dark gray cloak I stole from a dead neighbor before they took him away around my shoulders, I walk along the city wall, contemplating if I should take one solider up on his offer. He offered three gold coins if I show him my breasts. They're just tits, and the coins would buy me the papers I need.

The man who forges papers brings a new batch of them every night and makes rounds, looking for people who need them. He charges only two golds, so I'd even have one gold coin left over for supper instead of having to beg random people for a piece of bread.

Fine. Tits it is.

I stride toward the solider, and when he sees me, he whispers to his buddy and jerks his head my way. There's an alcove where the men urinate that's tucked nicely into the shadows. He walks there, and I follow him.

The second we get in, he leans against one wall and I against the other. Having no intention of removing my cloak, I part the heavy fabric and show him the handle of a knife peeking out of the pocket of my pants. The stench of urine makes my empty belly rise.

The soldier, maybe around nineteen years old, with green eyes darker than mine and fine blond hair, fumbles with his breeches, his weapons clicking and clanking.

I roll my eyes. "Take it easy. My tits aren't gonna run off." I'm turning forty-two in a few spans this cycle. It's not the first time a man has seen my tits, and hopefully won't

be last either. I want a child and a husband and a life somewhere near my sister.

This boy is a means to an end.

I need money.

He has it.

Breeches open, he's breathing heavily. He's cute,
bathed, fresh, young, and I'm thinking I might want to
seduce him for far more than for a few coins. He could get
me inside without papers. All he has to do is walk me in.

Suddenly, he pushes away from the wall and crosses the
distance to my side.

A hand gropes my breast.

I step back. "No touching."

He pins me against the wall, his lower body pressing
against mine, his hands roaming everywhere. I can't scream
for fear of being discovered and killed.

"Get back there, boy," I hiss.

He steps back and swings with a fist.

I duck, and he hits the wall behind me.

"You fucking whore," he hisses, also quietly because he
fears being discovered too. He's supposed to be on patrol.

I pull out my knife. "Get back."

He wrestles the knife out of my hand, and I try to
retrieve it, but the soldier's holding me, ripping at my
clothes, pulling the hood of my cloak away from my face.
When our eyes lock, I can almost see the desire in his. He
pauses, eyes wide, completely enthralled. I don't know how
to turn whatever this is off.

"You're so pretty," he says.

I knee him in the balls.

Bending, he curses, and I slip away and run smack into
a cloaked man blocking the alcove's exit.

The last time I saw a man wearing a cloak, he'd walked

into my inn and heralded the arrival of the savage horde that pillaged my village and killed everyone in it except my sister and me. They took us away from our home and forced us to join them on their destructive path, which reached all the way to the capital city of Lyan, where they set up their camp and where I last left them.

The tall cloaked man steps into the alcove. In a single swift movement, he grabs the solider by his neck and twists. A snap sounds, and the soldier crumbles to the floor, dead.

"Oh my king," I whisper and slap a hand over my mouth as the man bends to pick up my knife. He twists it in his palm, running a long red claw over the handle. There's only one creature with those kinds of claws. A savage from the horde.

He might've followed me. That boyish-looking one, what was his name? Neenei. Neenlei? Not sure of his name right now, but he was cute and kind to me, though I wasn't interested in him, thought I couldn't quite say why. Normally, I like good, kind men, unlike my sister. She likes dominant monsters. "Neensei?" I prompt.

The horde male snaps his head my way and says nothing, but under his deep brown cloak, his red eyes glow like beacons. A savage male for sure.

In a single step, he's on me, pinning me against the wall. I almost pee myself when he bends and sniffs my neck, his warm nose pressing against my skin. He snorts when he inhales, then licks my pulse.

One of my large breasts never made it back under my shirt. Naked and exposed, my nipple rubs against cloak.

Intent on kicking him and running away, I lift my knee, but he catches my leg and whispers at my ear, "Sometime later, I'll let you climb me like a tree and rub that sweet-smelling pussy all over me. Right now, be a good little girl and do what *kori* says." He brushes his lips over my earlobe and makes me shiver. "Nod that you understand."

I nod.

"For all they know, you killed a solider," he says.

"I didn't," I hiss, fear making my heart race.

"Nobody cares about you and what you did or didn't do, and nobody will believe a fae whore over a cute, reputable solider who died a tragic death at the prime of his life." The savage pauses, then says, "Keep nodding if you agree." He keeps me pressed against the wall, and his nose runs up and down my neck and shoulder as he sniffs me like a dog.

"What do you want?" I ask.

"For you to get us inside the city walls."

I snort, and then because laughter bubbles in my throat, I press my lips together, before I burst out laughing. I've probably lost my mind a little.

"If I could get past the soldiers at the gates," I tell him, "I would have."

The savage steps back and pulls out entry papers from inside his cloak. "You need these, and I have them. So we'll walk right in."

Reaching up, I yank back his hood. Many blond braids are pulled back and away to reveal a handsome, masculine, and rather clean-shaven face, apart from a patch of beard at the tip of his chin that he wears in a short braid. Long dark lashes frame red eyes ablaze with lust. A curved nose makes the savage's face masculine, and the full large lips soften the hard edges of his jaw and chin. He's smiling, showing me the tips of his sharp teeth. It's not Neensei.

"I hate to break it to you, Kori, but you've got red eyes and claws and the face of one of the savage males, and in case you haven't noticed, the king keeps the horde outside the city. Nod if you understand." Maybe he's crazy and thinks he's one of the king's people and can just walk past the gates. I haven't seen this male in Tolei's horde, and I've seen the entire horde.

The savage nods. "I understand. What I don't und—" He cuts off the conversation and presses a palm over my mouth. The savage's hearing is superior to mine, and he must've heard the soldier I'm just now hearing coming closer. Boots crush the gravel, and cigar smoke enters the alcove as the soldier lingers just outside.

"Moren," the solider whispers, no doubt calling his friend.

The savage turns up his nose, wiggles it.

"Moren," the soldier repeats.

I grab the savage's wrist and try to remove his hand from my mouth, but he won't let go. I bite, knowing this male won't yelp. He jerks his hand away and glares at me.

"Boy," I call out to the solider who's about to walk in on us and his dead friend. "It's kind of hard for Moren to answer with a mouth full of pussy. Ten golds to watch or keep walking."

The savage raises an eyebrow.

I bite my lip, worried the ploy won't work and the stupid kid will want to watch for ten coins.

"Hurry up, I have to piss."

The soldier's footsteps retreat until I can't hear him anymore. "You were saying?" I ask.

He shows me his palm, where blood trickles down and over the sigil on his wrist. "You bled me."

I didn't think I bit him hard enough to draw blood, but maybe this savage has thin skin or something. "You'll live, I'm sure."

"Can you heal it?"

He wants me to do magic again. I shake my head. "Please, go away."

"I searched for a fae. Any fae, but now that I've found a pretty fae, I'm going to take you with me."

He won't let up. "I can't get you inside the city. Been trying for spans to get in myself." Bending, I search the dead soldier for coins. I find twelve silvers, which amounts to one gold coin, in his back pocket and three golden ones inside his uniform.

Straightening, I prepare to leave. Picking up the savage's bitten hand, which is still bleeding, I drop a gold coin into it and close his fist. "For the trouble, and thank you for coming when you did."

"He would have hurt you," the savage says.

"I know."

"Why didn't you use your magic on him?"

"I don't have magic."

The savage frowns. "All fae have magic."

I tug the tip of my round ear. "I am not a fae."

The savage levels me with a look. "Baby girl, questioning my assessment of what I know you are isn't going to help you later when I bend you over my knee or a table or a bath, perhaps. I'll also decide on that later."

I look him in the eye. Too bad the fucker is two heads taller than me so I'm forced to crane my neck. "I wouldn't let you spank me for a hundred coins. There will be no later."

He runs a claw over my cheek. "I'm not offering you coins."

My turn to frown. "You're offering to pay me to get you inside, and it's not coins?"

The savage slides his hand under the cloak and pulls out half a dozen diamonds that he displays on his large palm. They're so shiny and pretty, and there're so many of them. A diamond collection like this one would buy me a tavern. Hell, maybe even a stable boy or a housekeeper. Maybe both.

I pick one up and roll it between my fingertips, feeling my body tingle. I put the diamond back and close his fist. "I would love nothing more than to take your fistful of shiny things that make my heart sing, but you want me to get you inside the city by doing some sort of fairy magic, and I'm telling you that I'm not a fae, and I can't do magic. If I take your diamonds and don't deliver on my end, you'll kill me. So, no, thanks. Keep looking and good luck."

I slip out of the alcove, feeling as if the male granted me a boon of freedom.

But he'll be back. This kind of male doesn't take no for an answer. READ MORE...

WANT MORE HORDE WHILE WAITING FOR ANOTHER SAVAGE? I HAVE a complete Alpha Horde series ready for a binge. Sample it for yourself on the next page.

ALPHA BREEDS TEASER

ALPHA HORDE BOOK 1

K ingsley

I GET MY PHONE AND ANGLE IT FOR A SELFIE. THE BRIGHT GLARE behind me is messing with my picture. I turn around in my chair and see something glowing on the floor. Oh, someone dropped their phone. Holding my cup carefully, I creep through the bushes to the fence, then set the cup down. This isn't a phone. It's a light coming out of thin air and expanding. "What the hell?" I slur. Someone must have slipped something into my drink. Fuck, I'm tripping. Better go back and sit in my chair.

I freeze and look around. I'm sitting on something soft. I look down and around, and it's a bed. A huge bed supported by a carved black headboard and footboard. It's a room, and it smells...sexy. My nipples perk. Holy crap, I'm turned on. Oh, shit, someone really slipped something into my drink. It's making my body buzz and making me see crazy things. How did I get here? I was just gonna go back and sit in the lawn chair. Where's my beer?

There's a single nightstand, brown sacks on the floor, and some animal rugs. I have no clue what happened. I don't see a door either. Nothing but dark green walls made of no material I'd ever seen before. They're deep green, almost black, with gray scratches and cracks that look like wear and tear. I dare not speak in case a serial killer drugged me and stashed me somewhere in his den. Or maybe he's got an underground house where he's gonna skin me and make clothes out of my hide.

I try not to breathe as I scoot over the covers. I swear these things are made of skin too. It's not cotton under my fingertips, the bedding feeing more like leather. I get to the headboard and prop my hands on it, then lean over to see the floor. It's something like cobblestone. Dungeon. Someone stashed me in their dungeon of horrors.

Or I could still be sitting in the green lawn chair and tripping about the dungeon. Oh man, this is some seriously fucked-up shit.

A click sounds, and the wall in front of me slides open.

My heart stops.

My breath ceases.

There is a monster at the door. A seven-foot-tall sage-green creature with pitch-black eyes, no ears—no ears!—a short nose, protruding cheekbones, and a forehead that blends with his scalp because he's bald on top. We stare at each other for what feels like forever. At least he's blinking. I'm not doing anything. I'm frozen and yet hyperaware my body is buzzing with something. It's as if ants are running all over my skin and making my nipples hard.

The monster lifts his face. His nostrils flare, and he tilts his head as if confused. On the bed, I back up and hit the headboard. Nowhere to run. He's blocking the only exit. When he steps inside the room, all bets are off.

I scream at the top of my lungs and spin around. At the wall behind me, sharp objects I recognize as weapons are stacked on the shelves. I grab the first thing I can reach, a sword, maybe, and swing. It falls at my feet. Too heavy. I grab something smaller and throw it. The sharp circular thing spins toward the monster.

He turns emerald green. Some sort of...body plates form over his body. They're like reinforcement plates for his abundant muscles, and they cover every inch of him. The sharp weapon I threw bounces off. I scream like a banshee, reaching for everything on the wall, throwing things at him, but he stands there as if I'm not even trying. Then he peels back his lips and shows me four sharp four-inch-long canines, a pair of them on each side of his mouth.

He opens said mouth. The sound that comes out is unlike anything I've ever heard, aside from horror movies, of course. I scream back, now in tears. "Oh my God, save me. Oh my God, what is that? Oh my God, this is the worst trip of my life. I swear I'll never take drugs or drink again. Please, please, take me to the hospital. I can't take this."

I sit on the bed, pull my knees toward my chest, and cover my head. I rock back and forth for a bit, then look up. Oh Lord, the monster is still there. At least his body is back to sage green. The emerald body plates no longer cover his muscles.

"I'm tripping hard," I tell him. "And I'm terrified. Is Jill around?" Monsters don't exist. He could be a frat boy I don't remember meeting, and I'm the crazy bitch in his bed who sees a monster instead a California boy-next-door in surfer shorts and flip-flops.

The monster speaks.

It's a language unlike any other, mostly hissing and growling. My throat and tongue can't produce these sounds, which leads me to believe I'm definitely on some hard-core drugs someone slipped into my beer. I gotta swim out of this and wake up.

The monster speaks again and moves away from the door. He motions with his hand. I think he wants me to leave. But I can't because I'm paralyzed on the bed, and I have no idea what's out there waiting for me. I'm afraid to get arrested. I'd lose my scholarship if that happened.

The monster stays quiet as he watches me. I hear a sound. It's barely audible. I think it's coming from him. It reminds me of the sound a rattlesnake makes when it shakes its tail. If he hisses at me, I will pee myself. "I don't understand you," I say and wipe my eyes.

He scratches his head, spins around, and I see his back. His hair starts in the middle of the back of his head. It's long and black, neatly braided down his spine. A pair of snakes are imprinted on his skin as glowing yellow tattoos. I'm making up some serious shit here.

The monster leaves, and the door slides closed behind him.

I'm alone in my own nightmare. My brain has conjured up monsters. The fear of losing my mind paralyzes me, and I grab the sheets and cover my body. I close my eyes and hope to God I sleep through this. Yes, I just have get through the trip until the drugs wear off. Then I'll find myself inside one of the frat boys' rooms, no worse for wear. Nobody's gonna hurt me. If the man who appeared in my mind as a monster wanted to hurt me, he would have. I'm just really messed up. That's all. Read more...

Also by Milana Jacks

Connect with me via email **HERE**

Read the Complete Horde Series:

#1 Alpha Breeds, #2 Alpha Bonds, #3 Alpha Knots, #4 Alpha
Collects

The Complete Hordesmen Series:

Hunger #1, Terror #2, Sidone #3, Fever #4, Dreikx #5, The Blind
Hordesman #6

Read the complete Tribes Series:

Marked #1, Stolen #2, Lured #3, Captured #4, Consumed #5,
Arked #6

Read the complete Beast Mates Series:

#0 Virgin - FREEBIE, #1 Blind, #2 Wild,

#2.5 Goddess, FREE via my Mailing List,

#3 Sent, #3.5 Their, #4 Caught, #5 His, #6 Free.

Read the complete Dragon Brotherhood:

Rise #1, Burn #2, Storm #3, Fight, #4

Short stories in IADB World: Jake 1.5, Eddy #2.5

Read the complete Age of Angels series:

Court of Command, #1 • Court of Sunder, #2 • Court of Virtue, #3

ΛBOUT THE ΛUTHOR

Milana Jacks grew up with tales of water fairies that seduced men, vampires that seduced women, and Babaroga who'd come to take her away if she didn't eat her bean soup. She writes sci-fi fantasy romance with dominant monsters from her home on Earth she shares with Mate and their three little beasts.

• She entertains readers on her mailing list as they await for books in the series. If you want in, join other readers at http://www.milanajacks.com/newsletter/ •

Meet me at
www.milanajacks.com

Made in United States
Troutdale, OR
08/10/2024

21912840R00105